T0006977

Advance praise for *Chola Salvation*

"In her first collection of stories set mostly in her hometown of East Los Angeles, Gonzalez unfurls the preoccupations of Mexicans and Mexican Americans and conveys an array of emotions they feel stemming from their blue-collar jobs, cultural heritage, faith and poverty. Her use of Mexican slang adds a distinctive flavor that enhances the atmospheric setting. Beneath the machismo and the matriarchal dominance that reverberate in Gonzalez's stories is a thriving Chicano/a pride that unites and rewards these flawed but resilient characters as they achieve bittersweet triumph over steep odds."   —*Booklist*

"Gonzalez's debut collection delivers a layered portrait of Mexican American life rooted in 1980s East Los Angeles. An inviting tapestry."   —*Publishers Weekly*

"Smoldering stories that center the lives of Mexican Americans by complicating common tropes and conceptions. This debut collection of interlocking short stories turns an unflinching eye on the small tragedies, gut-wrenching betrayals and enduring courage of working-class Latinx folks in East Los Angeles and the borderlands. Imagine *Winesburg, Ohio* featuring Chicanx of East Los Angeles with a touch of mystical realism."   —*Kirkus*

"What is most astonishing about *Chola Salvation* is Estella Gonzalez's skill in dropping the reader right into the action. Each story's razor-sharp characterizations allow us to recognize the bravada these *mujeres* live by, for better or for worse, or to root for queer love sought by *hombres*. With its bars, churches, hair salons and neighbors, this collection is East Los in its beautiful, aggrieved, celebratory finest."

—Helena María Viramontes, author of *Their Dogs Came with Them* and *The Moths and Other Stories*

Estella Gonzalez's work has appeared in *Kweli Journal, The Acentos Review* and *Huizache* and has been anthologized in *Latinos in Lotusland: An Anthology of Contemporary Southern California Literature* (Bilingual Press, 2008) and *Nasty Women Poets: An Unapologetic Anthology of Subversive Verse* (Lost Horse Press, 2017). She received a Pushcart Prize "Special Mention" and was selected a "Reading Notable" for *The Best American Non-Required Reading.* Her story, "Chola Salvation," won first-place in the Pima Community College Martindale Literary Prize and she was a finalist for the Louise Meriwether Book Prize for a collection of short fiction. She received her BA in English from Northwestern University and her MFA in fiction from Cornell University.

ESTELLA GONZALEZ

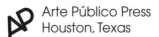

Arte Público Press
Houston, Texas

Chola Salvation is made possible through a grant from the National Endowment for the Arts. We are grateful for their support.

Recovering the past, creating the future

Arte Público Press
University of Houston
4902 Gulf Fwy, Bldg 19, Rm 100
Houston, Texas 77204-2004

Cover design by Mora Des!gn
Cover art by A.V. Phibes

Library of Congress Control Number: 2021930231

21 22 23   4 3 2 1

These *cuentitos* are for all the fierce chingonx in and outside East Los. *¡Órale!*

Table of Contents

Chola Salvation

I'm just kicking back, drinking my dad's Schlitz when Frida Kahlo and the Virgen de Guadalupe walk into our restaurant. La Frida is in a man's suit, a big baggy one like the guy from the Talking Heads but this one's black, not white. All her hair is cut off so she isn't wearing no braids, no ribbons, no nothin'. The only woman thing she has on are those hand earrings. I read in Mrs. Herrera's class that Pablo Picasso gave her those earrings because he thought she was a better painter than her husband.

La Virgen looks like my *tía* Rosa in the picture she sent to Dad. She has blonde hair, lots of white eyeshadow, and she's wearing chola clothes. You know, tank top with those skinny little straps, baggy pants and black Hush Puppy shoes. And she has on this lipstick like she just bit a chocolate cake. Her hair is so long, it touches the back of her feet. Her bangs are all sprayed up, like a regular chola, but she wears a little gold crown. A bad-ass *vata loca* sitting at the counter right in front of me.

At first, I don't recognize them but the moment I see Frida's unibrow and La Virgen's crown, I know. I really know for sure the moment Frida gives me a cigarette, even though there's this big ol' sign right at the counter saying, "Thank you

1

for not smoking." I suck on it while La Virgen holds up a lighter.

"*¿Qué ondas, comadre?*" Frida says, smiling. "Whassup?"

One of her teeth is missing and some of the others are all brown. No wonder she never smiles in her paintings. I don't know what to say, so I just take another swig from the beer I have behind the counter.

"Are you a shy girl?" La Virgen says. "Don't you know us, *esa*?"

"Man, sure I know you guys," I shout. I always shout when I'm a little buzzed. "You want some coffee or something?"

"*Un cafecito y un platillo de menudo.*"

"*¿Y tú, Friducha?*"

"How about some *pozole y unas cuantas tortillas de maíz,*" she says.

So, I serve them their menudo, pozole, tortillas and coffee. They tell me they're here to give me some advice: *unos consejos*.

"And believe me, you're going to need the advice, *preciosa*," Frida says. "Because your crazy Mami is going to let you have it with this whole *quinceañera* bullshit real soon."

La Virgen nods and takes another puff.

"We're here to tell you, you better watch out," La Virgen says. "So we have some rules for you to live by. You know, like those Ten Commandments Father Jorge taught you."

"Yeah, but this isn't about God, Jesus or some other Catholic laws," Frida says, ripping up her last tortilla.

"It's about you, homegirl, and about your *pinche* parents and this quinceañera they wanna force down your throat," La Virgen tells me. "You probably don't wanna hear it from me, especially since your mom is always throwing me in your face, saying how much you're hurting me every time you don't listen to her . . . but I want you to hear it from me, not something your mom picked up from your *abuela*."

I pull up a chair. I'm puffing away, the smoke relaxing me. I don't even feel sick, like those stupid films at school say you're supposed to. It's Sunday and Mom has been at church since 6 am. She usually stays away until about 10, because she sells *buñuelos* and tamales out in front of the church to people getting out of Mass. The restaurant's empty except for the three of us. I go over and lock the door, close the blinds, turn over the "Closed" sign and scooch a chair in between my *comadres*.

Frida leans over to me and takes my hand. La Virgen smiles with her chocolate brown lips.

"*Hermosa* Isabela, your parents say they just want you to be a 'decent' girl," Frida says. "They want you to grow up with all those bourgeoisie ideas. If you have to drink to protect your soul, then do it. Just stop with the cheap beer. You're better off drinking your father's *tequila*."

Then she pulls out a bottle of El Patrón Silver and three shot glasses. She fills the little glass to the top for me. I take it down in one gulp, and it burns at first, but soon I'm on my second shot, trying to keep up with La Purísima Virgen who's drinking the stuff like it's water.

"How 'bout another?" she asks, handing me another cigarette.

I notice her nails. They're painted blue, covered with little gold stars. It looks like she's holding a galaxy in her hands.

"How about taking up smoking?" Frida says. "*Sí*, I know I'm encouraging vices, but at your age you need all the help you can get. How about drinking? I have no idea when I started but before I knew it, I was challenging Leon Trotsky to tequila shots. *Pobre cabrón*, he was no match for me. Not even in bed."

Then she asks me if I'm still a virgin. When I tell her I am, she shakes her head.

"*Pobrecita* shy girl," La Virgen says. "What? Did your *mamita* tell you to wait 'til your husband popped your cherry?"

Man, she's rough. If she wasn't La Virgen, I'd just think she was another one of those high school skanks. But she's La Virgen. She knows everything and she's just telling it like it is.

"She told me only sluts had sex before they got married," I say. "Those types of women end up pregnant or *putas*."

They both look at each other and laugh again. Frida laughs so hard, she starts rolling around on the floor, kicking her feet. When she gets up, she's wiping tears from her eyes.

"Listen, *preciosa*," La Virgen says. "I don't know if you know this, but your little *pinche* saint of a mother had already started fucking your dad when she was fourteen. But she made the mistake of getting pregnant. Her *mamá, tu abuela*, hadn't bothered to tell her about what girls and boys can do when they're hot for each other."

"If you decide to take up with men, be careful!" Frida says. "Capitalist, communist, they're all the same. If you're not careful, you'll end up like me or, even worse, your mother. I loved a man, a great artist, who just couldn't respect me as a wife. 'Fidelity is for the bourgeoisie,' Diego would say. Well, thanks to the bourgeoisie, I painted the most miserable pieces of art ever. Maybe men aren't so bad . . . now that I think about it. Yes, men are another worthy vice."

Just then, the two of them start arguing over who's fucked the most men.

"Well, *cabrona*, you started like three thousand years before me," Frida gives in.

La Virgen smiles, sucks on her teeth and says, "Yeah, way before Johnny Cortez, I'd already had about 50,000 *papacitos*. Mmmm, maybe more."

"At least I had Trotsky," Frida says.

"And you're proud of that?"

Frida's unibrow scrunches up, and I think for sure she's going to throw her cigarette in La Virgen's face. La Virgen ignores her, makes a toast to men.

"*Ya, cállate*," Frida tries to shut her up. "Can we get back to helping Isabel?"

La Virgen laughs like she's won this one.

"Here are some more tips, homegirl," La Virgen says. "Listen up, *chica*, because we made them up especially for you."

Rule #1: Don't get pregnant. Have as much sex as you like, but don't get pregnant. Not until you really, really wanna. Believe me, I had four hundred sons and a daughter. That was a lot of work. What's worse is that this gang of three, some father, son and ghost, took over my gang while I was spending all my time raising these kids. Now look at this mess!

Rule #2: Go to school. You're gonna have to work the system. Why do you think I appeared like this little *virgencita* with the cutie pie face to Juan Diego and that fat bishop? I'm working this game, *chica*. Now, look at me. From Chiapas to Chicago, you see me everywhere: murals, tattoos, books, art. Yeah, Lupe's Ladies are all over. Like that crazy *vato* John Lennon once said about Los Beatles, "We're bigger than Jesus Christ."

Rule #3: You're in charge of your *panocha* and don't be afraid to protect it! Some guy is always gonna try to get into your pants, no matter how much you don't wanna. Even your sweet *papacito*. Yeah, don't think we don't know about him. If you have to kick some ass to teach him some respect, do it.

Rule #4: Spread the word. We need to get the word out to all our homegirls and our homeboys, especially the homeboys. Maybe they'll quit with all this macho shit they keep hearing from their families. I think Chuy and his *papá* may be causing all this.

Rule #5: We're all *indias*. Don't let your mom fool you. No one's a hundred percent. Be proud of the *indígena* inside of you. I know your old lady is down on you for behaving like an Apache, but believe me, we can't all be blonde and blue-eyed. Your mom heard the same lies about the white girls being the only ones worth anything from her own *mami*, a pure blood Tarahumara. Morena, you're beautiful too. Check my little brown self out one of these days, hanging in my gold frame right near the altar. I have the place of honor, not these other little wimpy Marías."

I'm wasted but I get the rules down. Suddenly, Frida puts her arm around me. She points to the paper skeletons I hung in a corner for Día de los Muertos.

"Look at those skeletons dancing. They're waiting for you, you know. Before you know it, you'll be fifty instead of fifteen and you'll wonder where your life went. Don't listen to those crazy sons of bitches you call your parents. You better start fighting them off now before you end up like those baby rats your mother found and drowned.

"Don't you have any friends, *muñeca*? That's strange for a girl your age, you know. At your age, I already had a boyfriend and was hanging out with my *clica*. If you had more vices, you wouldn't care so much."

Frida downs another shot of Patrón. Man, she wasn't even sweating.

"This is the most important thing I wanted to tell you: Ms. Herrera thinks you have a good eye for art. I bet you draw circles around your classmates. What do you think? Maybe art should be your vice. That would really drive your parents crazy, because they wouldn't understand. Smoking, drinking and fucking—those things they understand, because that's what they grew up with, that's what they lived. Art will be your world. You can create your own reality. Then you can escape this capitalistic quinceañera caca they're trying to feed you."

Frida lifts the bowl to her mouth and slurps the rest of her pozole. La Virgen takes another drag from her cigarette, drops it on the floor and stubs it out with her foot.

"Listen, *preciosa*, you'll probably think I'm a miserable pig, but you have to do something before your parents destroy you. Take this advice from me, La Friducha, whom you say you admire so much. Just forget about Father Jorge, all the *tías* and *tíos*, and just go with your gut. Believe me, you don't want the Pelona to get you while you're living some kind of middle-class hell. You'll thank me for it later."

Frida stands up and looks at her watch.

"Wait for me, *cabrona*," La Virgen says as she pulls out her compact mirror and puts on more chocolate brown lipstick.

"Just because you like going around painted like Bozo," doesn't mean I have to wait," Frida says. "We have other *carnalas* we gotta help."

"Hey, I'm not the one going around with a mustache over my lip and eyes."

"*Pinche puta*. You wanna take it outside?"

"*Tranquila*," La Virgen says. "I'm just kidding, homes."

They're leaving. I know if I ask them to stay, they won't. If they meet Mom, they'll kill her.

"We have to go," La Virgen says. "Another *carnal* needs our help. What? You never knew about my bad-ass chola side? Chica, in this crazy world sometimes you don't have a choice."

Before they leave, they both kiss me on the cheek. Frida hugs me real hard. La Virgen leaves me her last cigarette so I can remember her whenever I look at it. I see the brown lipstick mark where she sucked on it.

"*Adiós, muñeca*," Frida says. "Don't forget the rules."

I cry so hard after they leave because I know I won't see them for a long time. Just after they disappear, Mom shows up holding a white dress.

"*M'ija*, look what I bought you. Isn't it beautiful?" she says.

Mom's been shoving the whole thing in my face since I turned fourteen. She even gets the *tías* to nag me about it. Dad doesn't do it so much but he's starting to get on me about my weight. It never bothered him before, but now it's always, "Why can't you fix yourself up? Get out and do something. Pluck your eyebrows. What man is gonna want you?"

Yeah, I'm too fat and ugly for other guys, but not for him when he starts touching me in the shower or when he feels me up in the car. He never says nothing. He just looks at me the way other guys look at the girls at school. La Virgen's right. I have to protect my *panocha* even from my own dad.

Then, here comes Mom with her stupid quinceañera dress and all her dumb ideas about a big party with *mariachis* and everything. All that stuff costs, and I know they don't have the money. Even I know our crummy restaurant barely cuts it every month, now that there's a Pollo Loco on the corner.

Frida and La Virgen were right. Mom just wants to show off how well she raised me. Please. She can shove it. Just like that stupid white dress. Who told her to buy it anyway?

"Mom, I told you I don't want a quinceañera."

"But don't you want to wear this and look beautiful in front of your friends?"

"I don't have any friends."

"*Ay, no seas tan sangrona,*" she says, calling me stubborn and shoving the dress at me.

I throw it back at her and run back to the house. Dad doesn't even look up from his soccer game when me and Mom run right between him and the TV. I run into my room but can't lock the door in time. She just pushes the door real hard and busts in.

"*¡Niña malagradecida!*" she says. "Ungrateful brat! This dress cost me $300! Do you think I'm just going to throw it away?"

She still has the dress with her. As I try to hide in the closet, she grabs me by the shirt and starts slapping me.

Then I slap her back, and that's when she loses it. She takes a step back a little and then punches me in the gut. When I fall doubled over on my bed, she grabs me around the waist and sits me up. That *vieja* is strong for a short woman. It's her Tarahumara Indian blood. She's always bragging about how all her strength comes from her blood.

"*A chingao*, is that cigarette smoke I smell on you?" she grumbles, sniffing like a hound. "Where did you get them? Did you steal them from your father?"

I wait for her to slap me again, but she just picks up the dress and hangs it on the door. I lie down because I feel like barfing.

"You used to be such a good girl, so obedient, and now, *como un pinche apache!*"

She comes right up to me, leans over and tears down my Frida Kahlo poster, "My Birth." It's my favorite poster, and she knows it. But it's always bugged the shit out of her because it's not one of those pretty pictures of a puppy with big sad eyes or a ballerina girl. No, my poster shows a dead mother with a dead baby hanging out of her between her legs. It shows everything, even the mother's vagina covered in black pubic hair. What I really like about it is the painting of the Nuestra Señora de Dolores hanging over the bed. She's the real mother, because like all mothers, she's always in pain and makes everyone around her feel it. Mom calls it disgusting and starts ripping it into little pieces.

"There," she says when she's done. "Maybe you won't hit your own mother next time."

Before she leaves, she turns to the little bust of the Virgen de Guadalupe hanging over my door. I hear her say something stupid, like "*Ayúdame, Virgencita.*"

After she leaves, I lock the door, grab the bust and throw it out the window. That stupid dress. I wasn't about to look like a big white whale for her. Just because her *comadres'* daughters had theirs doesn't mean I have to go through this. She's not fooling me. This is about her. She wants to let everybody know her daughter's like all the other daughters, ready to get fucked. It's not bad enough that I'm fat and that everybody makes fun of me at home and at school, but now Mom wants to embarrass me in front of some crowd at church. Anyway, who's going to be stupid enough to be my escort? Tina's my only friend, and she dropped out of school last year and moved out to Coachella with her mom. So, I hardly see her.

Jesus, I haven't been to church for weeks now, so who cares? Dad never goes. He just stays home and watches soccer games. That's why I never take showers on Sundays. 'Cause I know the moment he hears the water running, he'll come right in to feel me up. One time I locked the door, and he got so mad, he almost broke the door down. When Mom got home, he told her some bullshit lie that I shouldn't lock the door because I might slip and fall, and nobody would be able to help me. Of course, Mom believed it. He says it's my fault because I'm fat. He's doing me a favor because no boy is gonna want some fat slob like me. He says it's my fault that Mom gets so mad at me, she won't fuck him. So I have to at least let him touch my tits and pussy. That's the only good thing for him about my being fat. At least I have big tits.

I grab some scissors out of my drawer and I start stabbing the dress. Then, before I know it, I cut it up into little pieces, even the big lace bow on the dress's butt.

I don't care. Just like Mom doesn't care about punching me in the belly or calling me a *pinche apache*. So what if it cost $300? Who asked her to buy it?

When I see all these little pieces of white on the floor, I freak out. They just sit there all shiny and white, staring up at me. I feel like I killed something.

I know it's a sign from the Virgen because the white shreds remind me of all the little stars on her hands. I've gotta get out. I feel real crazy and macho at the same time, like Dad when he gets drunk. This time I'm not gonna chicken out. This time, it's for real, and I'm not coming back. So I dig out some money from under my bed, pack up my duffel bag and jam to downtown LA. When I get to the Greyhound, I hide out in the bathroom until 2 in the morning and catch the first bus to El Paso.

～ · ～

I wake up the next day to a stinkin' pile of sweat. God does that fat lady smell. Her hair is all stringy and half her ass is over on my side of the seat. Yeah, she's fat like me. Maybe I stink too. That really bums me out. Maybe it's me that's smelling up this whole bus. I look over the seat in front of me. Naaah. Other people look like they stink too. The next stop, I'm gonna wash my pits just to make sure. I could use some of that fancy soap I stole from Mom. She always got pissed when I tried to use it. I loved the way it smelled, like that perfume in J.C. Penney's. It smelled even nicer than Dial.

I look at the fat lady's watch. It's barely 10. The guy at the bus station said we wouldn't get to El Paso until 8. Shit.

When the bus stops, at Blythe this time, I go wash my pits, my feet and my neck. This lady walks in. She's crying, looks like she's been punched in her eye. I pack my stuff up real fast.

"*M'ija*," she says to me, "you have some tissue?"

"Nah," I say. "There's some toilet paper here, though."

"Could you get me some?"

I get her some.

She's wiping her face, and her eye looks Chinese because it's all slanted and almost closed.

"Don't ever get married, sweetie," she says, like she's laughing.

I just try to walk real slow to the door.

"Don't ever marry a guy who drinks," she says. Now she's crying real hard.

12

"My dad drinks," I say, then I wish I'd kept my mouth shut.

"Yeah?" She turns to me. "So did mine."

I just get real scared when she tells me that. She sounds just like Mom. I feel like getting on that bus and driving it to El Paso myself. When I get back on, I sit way in the back, right next to the toilet, so I don't have to hear that lady cry. Jesus, when the hell are we getting out of here? Outside, it's just red rocks and hills, sometimes little bushes. There's barbed wire all over the place, as if anybody would want to climb over that. It's so fuckin' hot on the bus, but I won't take off my sweatshirt. I just have my muscle shirt on, no bra. I'm not try-ing to be sexy. I just forgot to take any bras with me. Anyway, I see this slimy guy look at me weird. . . . I don't need any-body hassling me right now. Of course, when the bus gets going and I get up, some asshole has to say something.

"Hey, fat ass, can you get your stomach out of my face?" some old woman says.

"Fuck off," I say. "I'm just trying to get my duffel bag."

The stupid lady punches me in the gut. I fall over on the guy who gave me that weird look. He cops a feel when I try to get up. I almost pop him one, when the bus driver stops the bus.

"Hey, you! Don't start any trouble or I'll leave you right here."

I roll my eyes real hard, grab my duffel bag and head back to my seat. *What else can I do?* The last thing I need is for him to leave me here in the middle of nowhere or maybe call the cops. After digging around my bag, I find the picture of Tía Rosa sitting on her boyfriend's lap. She's holding a cigarette. Looks like he's squeezing her. A big margarita glass sits on the table next to them. She's laughing. Her lips are red-red, like a Crayola crayon, and her hair is short and gold, like Blondie's.

On the back of the picture she wrote: "*Con mucho cariño y amor para mi sobrina Isabela, de parte de tu Tía Rosa. Aquí estoy con mi novio Pablo en el restaurante Ajúúa! Visítame cuando quieras. Mi número de teléfono es 13-16-57. Mi dirección es Avenida 16 de Septiembre 3555, Juárez. Los espero.*"

That's her address: Avenida 16 de Septiembre in Juárez. I wonder if she wanted to invite all of us, or just me. I guess she thought I'd be coming with Mom and Dad. I don't think she really liked Mom, though. One time, at a party, Tía was dancing to a *cumbia*, "*Tiburón, Tiburón,*" with Uncle Beto. She looked like that statue of Our Lady of Fatima with her small angel lips, dark eyes and pale skin. She wore her short blue dress. Mom was in the kitchen serving the *carne asada* Dad had just cooked up outside.

"*Vieja sinvergüenza,*" she said when I walked in with all the paper plates. "Your aunt just likes shaking her butt in front of everybody."

"She's a good dancer."

"She should be helping me in the kitchen."

"Where's Tía Amelia?"

"She's helping your father cook the steaks."

A little while later, I saw Uncle Beto taking Mom by the hand and trying to make her dance. Mom laughed, shook her head. Dad tried to take out Tía Rosa, but she said no and walked outside to the patio. Instead of going back to the party, he came after me, but I split into the patio with Tía Rosa. She was sitting there smoking and singing, "*Zandunga.*"

"*¿Qué pasa, muñeca?*" she said.

I could smell her Coco Chanel perfume mixing with the smoke. "Nothing."

"Want a cigarette?"

"Yeah!"

I took a little puff. I still believed my dumb health teacher when she said smoking made you sick. I didn't want to embarrass myself in front of Tía, so I just made sure not to breathe in too deeply. We just smoked and listened to all my other aunts, uncles and cousins whooping it up in the house. I just wanted to sit there and smoke forever. Tía just kept singing until Uncle Beto came out looking for her.

"I'll be there in a minute," she said, lighting up another cigarette. "What a pain in the ass."

"Can I have another one?"

"Already? Why are you smoking so much? You're only thirteen."

"I don't know. I just hate being here."

"Me too."

Tía started singing another Mexican song. Beto came out again, and this time she got up. After a while, Mom came out looking for me and told me to "play" with my cousins. Jesus, I was thirteen. It's not like I was playing with *pinche* Barbies. I went back into the house and the first thing I saw was Dad dancing with my baby cousin Evelina. At first, I couldn't believe it was him. Everybody was dancing real fast and jerky to a *cumbia*, but he was dancing slowly so he wouldn't step on Evelina's little shoes. I remember I wanted to cry so bad, I ran into the kitchen, grabbed a beer out of the fridge and just sat outside waiting for everybody to leave.

Before Tía left, she gave me another cigarette and asked me to go visit her. That was before she and Uncle Beto divorced. After the divorce, Mom never let me go and visit her. Dad told me the same bullshit that Tía Rosa was a *vieja sinvergüenza*. Uncle Beto married some other woman he'd met at a cabaret and didn't visit us anymore.

No big loss. I never liked the fucker anyway.

I can see from the bus window that outside it's getting brighter and hotter. I break out my notebook and start drawing an old chola with big feathered hair. First, I draw her skinny, then I draw her fat like me, with big boobs coming out the sides of her muscle shirt. When I look up, everything looks melted. I close my eyes and try to forget about the stink and the crying. I pretend like I'm dead and I finally go to sleep.

～∙～

After getting to El Paso and crossing the bridge to Juárez, I take a bus I think goes by Tía's house. I get off on September 16th Street, right where the bus driver tells me. All I smell is rotten mangoes and car fumes. It's so hot out here, and my pits are already dripping. God, I forgot how poor everybody is here, especially the *indios* and the little kids. Mom was always hassling me about throwing me out with the *indios*. There ain't that many in East LA. Now I know why she thought it was a big deal. Jesus, they're really poor. I see a mother and kids sitting on the sidewalk. She's dividing up what the kids have brought in begging.

I once knew a guy named Indio. All the kids used to call him that. I think his real name was Arturo. He used to hang out with all the other winos on the corner of our block.

"*Pinche indio,*" Dad used to say. "All they ever do is beg and drink. They don't know the meaning of work."

I always wanted to ask Dad why he said that. Mom was half Tarahumara and I know Grandma, Dad's mom, was pure *india*. One time when I braided my hair just like Laura Ingalls on "Little House on the Prairie," he called me a *pinche india fea*. He was pissed. I look at my braids now. They're like the baskets I see for sale on the sidewalk.

God this place is dirty. I don't want to look at the little Indian girl with her little brown girl face selling chiclets in her yellow dress so bright she looks like a sun. She walks back to her mom, who's now sitting on some steps. The woman starts yelling at her.

The little girl runs back to me. Poor kid. Her mom probably beats the shit out of her if she doesn't sell enough of those stupid little gums.

"*Niña, dame dos paquetitos.*"

I give her a quarter, even though I know I better save my money. I hope I don't have to stay at some motel or something. What should I tell Tía? Should I tell her about Mom and the dress? What if she sends me back to LA? I hope she doesn't make me go back. What if she calls the police? Then I'm booking it, because there's no way I'm staying in a Mexican jail! Well, if I can't stay here, I'm going to Mexico City and visit Frida's house. Maybe I can hide out there for a little while. At least I can see that before I have to go back. Jesus, I don't think I can hold out until I'm eighteen.

Maybe if I told Tía about Mom punching me? But then I'd have to tell her why. Shit. Maybe she'll understand because she hates Mom too. I think she does. I wonder if she knows Mom thinks she's a slut. I don't know if I can tell her about the dress. Jesus, it stinks here. Or maybe it's me. I haven't showered in days. Maybe I should tell her about Dad. I can't believe I'm here. I hope I don't have to go back. Mom'll kill me for sure.

"*¡Oye, mamacita!*" a male voice slurs.

I keep walking real fast.

"*¡Tú! ¡Gordita!*"

I see some guy with a cowboy hat waving at me. Jesus fuck. Now he's walking alongside me.

"*Bonita, ¿estás sola? ¿Quieres un novio?*"

He looks at me the way Dad does when he feels me up. Cowboy guy has a skinny Pedro Infante mustache and he's wearing this thick belt with a huge belt buckle like Dad wears. Shit, my shirt's all sweaty and I know I stink that fat stink. But fuck this, not this time. I'll pop him with my duffel bag if he gets any closer. Cowboy guy's voice sounds far away but he's still walking right behind me, making kissing noises. God, I don't wanna faint out here. I spot a church and walk in real fast.

It's nice and cool but it's so fucking dark. I can't see anything except the altar. I book it right up the middle, sit right up in front with some old ladies and bow my head like I'm praying. I just whisper, whisper, whisper, look around. I don't see him. Then this old lady next to me starts poking me with her elbow.

"I know you're not praying, *esa*," she says. I look at her hands and see those little stars on the nails.

"Virgencita," I sigh. "You scared me. I thought you were one of these *viejas*."

"Hey, some of these *veteranas* are my homegirls," she says.

She's wearing a black rebozo but I can see the little points of her crown sticking up on her head, through the black.

"Virgen," I say, "you have to help me."

She takes me to the side of the church where all the short candles are in front of a saint's statue.

"*¿Qué pasa?*" she says.

"It's this cowboy guy," I say. "He's after me." I start to cry. I don't know why. I hardly ever cry.

"Is he after your *panocha*?"

"Yeah," I say. "He was making kissing noises and calling me 'Mamacita.'"

"Let's go."

When we push the door open, I see him right there, across the street from the church.

"He's right there," I tell the Virgen, "with the cowboy hat."

She starts crossing the street and does one of those shrill whistles, with her fingers in her mouth. It's so loud I can hear her even when a big bus passes right in front of me. Cowboy Dude smiles his little mustache smile and starts walking over to us. La Virgen looks him up and down, like some guy she's about to dance with. La Virgen whips off her *rebozo* and hands it to me. Something shiny sticks out of her pants. It looks like a gun. When she pulls it out, it looks just like that gun in the Dirty Harry movies. Everybody clears out, even the little *indio* kids. Cowboy dude just stops still, drops his little smile. La Virgen starts waving her *cuete* around in front of Cowboy Dude's face, then she puts it right up to his mouth.

"*Bésalo,*" she says, telling him to kiss it.

Cowboy Dude just opens his mouth like he's gonna say something.

"*Bésalo, cabrón,*" La Virgen says and cocks the gun.

Her tiny finger doesn't look strong enough to squeeze the trigger, but I know she can pop that *cuete* faster than any cowboy. Cowboy Dude puckers up and kisses the gun. A little kiss.

"*Como besas a tus mamacitas,*" La Virgen says, meaning, "Like you're in love."

He kisses it again. This time though, he frenches the barrel.

La Virgen smiles, puts her *cuete* back in her pants. Cowboy Dude's legs keep shaking even as we start to walk away. Suddenly, he tries to jump her but only falls down screaming. He's grabbing his crotch and rolling around on the sidewalk. La Virgen looks back at Cowboy Dude, spits right on his face and gives him a good kick in the ribs. All of a sudden, there's a crowd of *indias* around us with their little kids. Some of them are laughing and making the sign of the cross on their heads and chests. Down the block, there are a couple of Mexican cops staring.

La Virgen takes back her *rebozo*, now green and covered with gold stars. "Keep this," she says, handing me the huge gun.

I stick it in my duffle bag as she grabs my arm and pushes me across the street, straight into a purple taxicab.

"Templo Chola Tattoo," La Virgen tells the cab driver. "You're gonna need it," she says, lighting up a cigarette for me.

"Here, drink some of this," she orders, handing me a bottle of Hornitos tequila.

I take a little sip and almost throw up.

I can see the cab driver staring at La Virgen every time we stop. Hasn't he ever seen a chola before? When we get to the tattoo place, Frida's waiting for us at the front door. This time she's dressed in a long skirt and her hair's braided up and wrapped around her head.

"*Hola, muñeca*," she says hugging me.

I almost fall, I feel so dizzy. "How come we're here?"

"Because your *tía* works here," Frida says.

Inside, I see the blonde woman in my picture working on this big, fat guy's back. She's wearing glasses, and he's wearing thick black shades so tight, a little bit of fat hangs over them. I see some women sitting down next to the white, white walls. All around, cartoon pictures hang. My head feels like it's buzzing. It's so bright inside, I want to shut my eyes.

"*Hola, amores*," Tía Rosa says, not looking up from the fat guy's back. "*Ahoritita les ayudo.*"

All I can hear is the needles buzzing. Two other guys are helping my aunt. I think one of them is her boyfriend Pablo, because he has his long black hair in a ponytail and doesn't look old like Uncle Beto or Dad.

"Frida?" Tía Rosa says. "Lupe? Who do you bring me?"

Tía Rosa knows my *comadres*? I guess she would know them.

"We bring you Isabela," Frida says. "She needs a tattoo, maybe two, to save her."

"Save her from what?" Tía Rosa says.

"From her mother and your brother Rodolfo," Frida says, pulling out a big black book from behind Pablo.

Tía Rosa finally looks like she recognizes me. She grabs my arm and takes us into a back room. On the walls she has pictures of La Virgen and little candles everywhere. On one side is a poster of Frida with a skull on her forehead. I can tell Tía smells the tequila on my breath as she gets in my face, looking closer. She lifts her hand and caresses my cheek.

"Did he touch you?" she asks.

I nod and start to cry like a baby. Then I unload, telling her everything about Mom, the dress and Dad. She gives me some water mixed with sugar.

"You gave her too much tequila," Tía says.

"It was Lupe," says Frida.

"She'll need it, if you're gonna give her a tattoo," La Virgen says.

"We'll do that later," Tía says.

I want to get a tattoo so bad, but I pass out before I can look through the book Frida hands me.

⤙⤚

"Why did ya come over to this hellhole?" Mousy says.

We're watching the hookers walk up and down the street in front of the nightclubs, trying to find johns. I see the little

Indian girls begging the American tourists for money, trying to put on their sad faces, making their little lips puffier and sadder. I can smell old meat and blood from the butcher shop next door.

"I don't know," I say. "Tía lets me smoke as much as I want to. Anyway, she says she'll teach me how to be a tattoo artist."

"You could have learned that back in East Los," she says, passing me her roach.

"No thanks," I say. I tried it once and it made me feel like shit. I think it was laced with Angel Dust or acid or some homemade shit. I'm not chancing it anymore. I'm sticking to cigs and booze, for now.

"At least my old man can't feel me up in the shower anymore."

"Your old man did that? *¡Pinche asqueroso!*"

We can hear Mousy's grandfather playing his accordion in La Rondalla club. His name is Don Ramón and he still plays even though he's pushing eighty. It's sad seeing that old man holding that heavy old accordion and pushing its buttons. Don Ramón is accompanied by two friends so old, they look like they're gonna bite the dust real soon. He has to support Mousy and her mom while her dad's out in California. Supposedly he'll send money back to them. For now, Mousy works at the laundry, washing and ironing clothes. Shit, I'd rather go to school than burn my hands washing clothes in Clorox.

"What time is it?" I ask Mousy.

"It's almost time for the *brujas* to come out."

"I better get back to the house, or Tía's gonna yell at me again for not getting to school on time."

"You're lucky. I have to get my ass out to the laundry by 5."

"See you tomorrow, homegirl."

When I walk into the house, my cousins are wearing out the Atari I got real cheap last week at a secondhand store in El Paso. Noel keeps bugging me for a Walkman, but I can't get one for cheap like the other stuff. Evelina always wants a *saladito* from the corner store. I walk to the kitchen and warm up a tortilla. There's a scorpion on the wall, so I break out the heavy huarache Tía uses to kill them. She won't use Raid because it stinks. Yeah, this whole place is worse than my place in LA, but at least Tía doesn't treat me like some punching bag or her personal *puta*. I even take showers on Sundays now.

As soon as I walk into the kitchen, I see Pablo looking through some of my drawings I left on the table. I feel my stomach getting all tight and I start sweating. Why do guys think they can do whatever they want? Why can't they keep their fuckin' hands to themselves? So I grab the *cuete* out of the duffel bag. Shit, I forgot how heavy it was. That's okay. I can use two hands like that Angie chick does on *Police Woman*.

"Freeze, motherfucker!" I say, real tough, pointing the big ol' gun at his head.

Poor Pablo. I think he's gonna shit right there. He puts the drawings down real slow.

"*Cálmala*," he says. "I was just looking at your drawings, *esa*. Your *tía* asked me to do a tattoo for you, so I thought I could use one of these."

I don't know if I'm just surprised or what. Before I can think, I drop the stupid gun, and I'm lucky it doesn't go off, because the police down here don't fuck around.

Pablo's cool. He doesn't freak out about the whole thing, but I know my *tía*'s gonna trip. Pablo lets me keep my gun and promises not to go through my stuff again without my permission.

"Keep it in Templo's backroom," he says. "That way the kids won't get to it."

Shit, I forgot about my cousins.

I follow him out to the tattoo parlor and stuff the Virgen's gift in the drawer of the little table where Tía keeps crap, like pencils, old 8-track tapes and other stuff. I ask Pablo to tattoo La Virgen in her chola clothing on my shoulder. He's never seen her like I've seen her, so I draw a quick sketch of her.

"Hmmm," he says, looking at my drawing real close.

Can he do it? Or does he think my drawing's a piece of crap? I'll really shoot him if he tells me that. Instead, he gives me a paper cup with some yellow stuff.

"Drink it . . . a little mescal," he says.

The tattooing burns like hell, and even the mescal doesn't help. What keeps me goin' is that Pablo tells me Tía wants to teach me how to handle a needle so I can do my own tattoos, maybe work with her and Pablo here in the Templo.

"*Órale, esa*," Frida says when I tell her about Tía teaching me how to tattoo. "Let me see your arm."

At first, I feel all proud about my crazy Virgen.

But Frida throws my arm down and growls, "What about me, *cabrona*? When the hell are you gonna put me on your arm?"

Fuck, I didn't know artists could get so pissy. But she's my *carnala*, and I owe her some blood. So now, I have the Virgen on my left shoulder and La Frida on my right. The next one I'm getting is the old lady I drew on the bus. She has big feathered hair and is holding her big *cuete*, almost as big as La Virgen's. She's dressed in Frida's suit and one of those old-school hats with two peaks. On her shades, you can barely see this wanna-be Pedro Infante guy she's getting ready to shoot.

"That's a *firme* tattoo, *esa*," Mousy approves.

I'm standing next to her, trying to fill in the *rebozo* on her "Adelita" tattoo. It's so hot in the salon, I'm just wearing my bra and muscle shirt. Tía doesn't care and, besides, I want to show off my tattoos.

"Is it the Virgen de Guadalupe?"

"Yeah, but she's different. See? No cutie-pie face for her."

"She's blonde?" Mousy says, like I made a mistake when I drew her.

"She's a chola, *mensa*. She's just dyed her hair, but she's still a *morena*."

Mousy moves her head closer to my shoulder. "Oh, check it out," she says. "She's wearing Dockers and everything."

"Yeah, she's one of us, a *vata loca*."

"Who did it for you?" Mousy says.

"Pablo, but I drew it first. See my picture? It's right up there, next to the jaguar. It's in the black frame next to my Frida Kahlo."

"Who's Frida Kahlo?"

"She's my *comadre*," I say. "She saved my life. See, she's on my other arm."

Mousy's my third tattoo since I started at Tía's salon. I've been working on her "Adelita" tattoo for two hours already and I'm still not finished. I have to finish her before I catch the bus to El Paso. Then I have to do my homework and get my lunch ready. Shit. I have so much to do. Plus, I need a cig. Tía won't let me smoke inside the salon because she wants to keep the place sanitary. It's not a toilet, she tells me.

The phone rings. I know it's Mom again, trying to get me to go back home. No way. She says if I don't go back home, they'll come and get me. Go ahead and try. I go back to my tattooing and forget them.

I'm trying to fill in Adelita's hair. I'm so into it, I don't hear anything except Diana Ross breathing heavily on "Love Hangover" over the speakers. Then I smell garbage and rotten meat from the butcher shop next door. I think it's Maritza who's opened the front door because she's my next appointment, and she wants a bleeding heart on her tit.

"¡*Cabrona!*"

It's Dad. He's wearing his Dodgers cap and he's standing in front of the open door. He looks half asleep, his eyes bloodshot. Don't know if it's the trip or if he's been drinking. My stomach feels real tight, and I want a cig real bad.

"Get in the car," he says, jerking his head.

Shit. Where's Frida? Where's the Virgencita?

"Who's that?" Mousy says.

"Dad."

"Motherfucker."

I see Frida walk up to my mother and lean into the car window. Mom just sits there like the car's still moving. I want La Virgen to come in and make Dad French her gun like Cowboy Dude. I want her to pop that *cuete* until teeth, blood and pieces of lip fly out of his head. But she's nowhere to be seen. Not this time. Frida's just leaning against the car, smoking a cigarette. Is she still mad about the Virgen tattoo?

"Isabela!" he says real hard.

It's like that time I put my hands up to cover my tits in the shower before he grabbed them. He walks right up to me. And I make like to ignore him and just keep working on Mousy's tattoo. I hear him suck in his breath when he sees the tattoos on my shoulders.

"¿*Me oístes, cabrona?*" he says, grabbing my hair.

I almost stab Mousy in her eye. She gets up real quick and runs to the back room.

The next thing I know, I'm drilling that needle right into his hand. He gives me a good slap on the ear as he backs off. I've still got the needle.

"Rudolfo! *¡Por Dios!*"

It's Mom. She's standing at the door with Frida and La Virgen.

"Get out," he says. "Get back in the car."

"Isabela," Mom says, wiping her red face. "He misses you."

"The only thing he misses is grabbing my tits."

I'm looking at Mom straight in the eye. Mom blinks like she doesn't understand. She's worse than a kid. More like a baby, same as Dad. She starts saying something about Tía forcing me to stay with her, changing me into some *puta* so that everybody can laugh at her. Her hands open and close, open and close.

"If anybody's gonna turn me into a *puta*, it's Dad," I say looking at him.

Dad's mouth hangs open. "*Hija de la chingada*," he says and whips off his belt.

That's when I know he's drunk because he always acts like a *puro macho cabrón* when he gets *pedo*.

"Go ahead," I say. "I'm sick of you treating me like I'm your little whore."

"Don't say that, Isabela!" Mom cries.

Dad comes at me again. This time I grab one of those big candles, one with the picture of the Virgen, and I smash it on his head. There's glass and blood all over the place. I feel like throwing up and choking at the same time. Dad just looks at me like he doesn't know who I am. Blood drips down from all over his head to the floor.

"You're not my daughter anymore," Dad vows.

"So?"

"Don't ever come back."

"Fuckin' straight, I won't."

He reminds me of "Carrie" with all that blood covering his face. Mom just keeps crying. I can't understand what the hell she's saying. I grab another candle, just in case. . . . Mom and Dad turn and start walking out the door. They don't even look back at me.

Mousy comes up to me. She's holding my gun. I laugh because it's too late, and she's not holding it right. It's so heavy Mousy can't even lift her hand. I guess they never showed *Police Woman* down here. I stick it in her pants and cover it with the top of her shirt.

"Keep this for me, *vata*," I say. "I may need it later."

She tries to get me to the back room, but I just wanna sit down on my barber chair and watch Mom and Dad drive away. I wait for Frida and La Virgen, but I know I'm not gonna see them again for a long time. After about five minutes, I go to the door and turn over the "*abierto*" sign.

I Hate My Name

———

I hate my name. What the hell does Lucha mean anyway?

"To fight," Grandmother Merced tells me.

"To kick ass," Tía Suki once told me.

But really, it's just a name most people make fun of. George, my boyfriend, tells me I should change it to Lucy, just like he changed his name from Jorge to George. But everybody's always known me as Lucha.

"*Que Lucy ni que nada,*" Merced told me when she overheard me talking to George on the telephone. "Your mom gave you that name, and you have to stick to it."

Actually, Merced gave me my name. I know this because Tía Suki told me so on her last ever visit to Merced. We were sitting in the kitchen. I remember because I was near death with the flu and was just getting over it. Suki had promised to make me a *caldo de albóndigas*. And I remember feeling hungry for the first time in a week when I smelled the meatballs cooking in the thick soup.

"*Ay*, Lucha," Suki said. "More and more you're looking like Merced."

Great, I thought. Not only do I have a crappy name, now I'm starting to look like an old hag. Merced is the last person I wanted to look like ever.

"Is the soup ready?" I asked Suki. "All Merced ever makes for me these days is Spam and eggs. Or beans."

"Almost," Suki said, lowering the flame and dipping her big spoon into the soup. "Merced likes her *albóndigas* right away, too."

I just wanted to eat and go back to bed so I could dream about George and his beautiful hair and eyes. When Suki put the bowl in front of me, the *albóndiga* soup steamed up into the ceiling with its peeling paint. I didn't wait for Suki to serve herself before I started slurping up the hot broth. The more meatballs I ate, the better I felt.

"Just like Merced," she laughed, looking at me. "You know she's the one who named you?"

I just looked down at an *albóndiga*, a big brown boat in a sea of rice, cilantro and potatoes. I kept eating.

"She named you after your mom left Don Pedro," Suki said, then slurped her soup.

Merced had told me about Mom and Don Pedro, this guy Mom had met at El Yuma Bar. She ran off with him to Bakersfield without telling Merced. He had been way older than Mom, but I think that's why she liked him, because he was old and quiet. Not like Merced, skanky and loud. But they hadn't lasted, and soon she was back, dragging me back from Bakersfield.

"But she hadn't named you yet," Suki told me, handing me a tortilla. "She just called you *muñequita*. I kind of liked that."

I tried to finish my *albóndigas* quickly so I could go to bed with my thoughts of George. Suki's voice was low and deep and crawled into my ears, then into my brain. Before I could finish eating, she told me that one day, when she had come to drop off some *yerbas* from her garden, she had found

Merced and her neighbor Rufina in the living room, singing to some *ranchera* singer.

"Lucha Villa," Suki told me. "Merced and Rufina were singing '*Amanecí en tus brazos.*'"

Merced was holding a picture of Leandro in one hand and me in the other. Yeah, *pura novela*, but I believe it. She's been in love with that guy for so long, I don't think she'll ever get over him.

"Lucha still sings," Suki went on. "Not as good as Lola Beltrán, but she is good."

"She still sings," I repeated, rolling up the last tortilla in my hand. "Good."

"And beautiful too," Suki said. "Long black hair. Brown skin."

I stopped eating. I knew what Suki was trying to do, and it wasn't going to work. No way was I falling for that Chicano pride crap. I knew better. That shit was over. This was the 80s and I was an American. So, over the soup I whispered, "Lucy," and watched my breath and steam float up into the peeling paint. Next year, when I started at Roosevelt High School, I would start using my American name, just like George. I would make the teachers remember my name and soon, I knew, Merced would call me Lucy too.

~≈~≈~

The minute I walk in, it hits me—Aqua Net hairspray and Miss Clairol or whatever they use in this cheesy salon to color hair. César's Hair Salon always looks empty when I walk by on my way to Griffith Junior High, but today it's totally full of so many yapping *viejas* and blaring music. It sounds like a party. Some of the women, mostly old ladies like Merced, are gossiping while they wait and rip through hair books. Some are in the back, getting their hair washed, lying back in their chairs like their heads have been cut off. Other women sit in big fat black chairs, white plastic helmets on their heads. From the boom box sitting on the counter next to the cashier, I hear Los Bukis' singing "*Me muero porque seas mi novia.*" It's almost like a disco in here with big mirrors shaped like stop signs hanging against walls covered in foil wallpaper with black and red velvet flowers.

I drop right next to a woman reading a *novela* with pictures of women in bikinis and big eyelashes. I don't know why I'm here except that I don't know where else to go to get the haircut I want. Ever since I can remember, it was either Merced or her neighbor Rufina who cut my hair, and always in the same boring style, with my long hair to the shoulders and straight-up bangs. I am so sick of my flat little-girl hair—the Lucha hair. I want something for Lucy. American Lucy. At first, I think maybe I can get my hair permed like Brooke Shields or some other cool movie star, but then I remember this girl in my history class who got one and she just looked like a walking Brillo pad. So now, that's what everybody calls her.

The boys call out to her: "Hey, Brillo! Comb your hair." "Brillo, need a perm?"

It's awful, but I don't say anything. If I do, they'll come after me. So when a hairstylist with hair the color of mangoes comes up to me and asks what I want, I point to the feathered model in the *Women's Style of the 80s* hair book. She introduces herself, but I can't hear her name over the chatter and the *norteño* music. I show Mango the picture of the woman with the Farrah Fawcett feathered hair. This is the style I want to wear in September when I get to Roosevelt.

"Hmm," Mango says, "La Farrah."

"*Sí,*" I say, "La Farrah."

Only, this will be La Lucy, and I have to do it before Merced gets back from the hospital and figures out that I took ten dollars from her purse.

Mango leads me to the little black sinks and wraps a towel around my neck. She leans me back. The water feels hot but I don't say anything. When Mango starts rubbing in the shampoo, she looks down and asks me about Merced. I can barely hear her through the water rushing over my ears. She says something about Merced's hair and when is she going to come back to get her hair done. I want to tell her that Merced now uses Miss Clairol's "Turkish Night" and her hair isn't mango-colored anymore. Now it's black-black, like Elvis' hair. It's so black it doesn't even shine. And she has Rufina cut it in the middle of the kitchen with newspapers laid out on the floor.

I don't say any of this, so I just smile and close my eyes while Mango rinses my hair. I try not to think about Merced, only of Lucy. Everything feels soft. Even the hard plastic against my neck melts under me. Before I know it, Mango is straightening me up, wrapping a towel around my head, squeezing it a little to get the extra water out. She walks me over to one of the clear plastic chairs facing a stop-sign mirror, Los Tigres del Norte singing "*Un día a la vez.*"

"Ready?" she says, smiling.

I nod and smile back.

A black cape whips around my neck, and Mango takes out a comb with a thin pointy handle, combs my hair flat against my skull, and her scissors start flashing under the fluorescent lights. Black chunks fall around me, and my head feels lighter. The feathered model's face floats around me. Yes, I nod. Yes. Soon I'll have my American hair.

"Hold still, *m'ija*," Mango says, holding my face still between her soft wet hands.

They remind me of my boyfriend George's hands on my face when we kiss. I imagine him kissing me, my new feathers looking good against his shiny brown hair.

Mango starts cutting again, her face close to mine. I look at her hair, little dried wisps like the fibers that stick out of the mango's pit when you're done sucking on it. If I would reach out from underneath my cape, I know I could break the ends off. I close my eyes, waiting for my feathers to spread out. I can hear Mango rattling around in her little black drawer. When I look, she's pulling out a big round yellow brush. The hair dryer revs up, whining like a little airplane. I can feel Mango rolling my hair around the brush, pulling, burning my scalp.

Then, what I've been waiting for: she pulls out the smaller round brush from the pile in her drawer. The bristles scrub against my skin, pulling my hair by the roots, drying under the noise. Suddenly, the blow dryer stops. I keep my eyes closed, knowing that when I finally open them, I'll see the model from the hair book in the mirror. The blades squeak in my ear, cut more of my hair. And then, the blow dryer starts again. And it's like this for the next half hour: first the blow dryer, then the scissors. Dry, cut, dry, cut—the rhythm scares my eyes open.

I almost scream. The hair on my right side is thicker and longer, one perfect wing tucked against my head. The other is so short, my ear looks like a little *saladito*. Instead of the beautiful Farrah model, I see a Cabbage Patch doll with a fat face and a balding head. Shit. American Lucy is screwed.

I can just hear it now: "Hey, Cabbage Patch, where's your hair?" "*Saladito* ears! You need a lemon or what?"

"I need to trim the other side," Mango says.

Good thing the cape keeps my hands from reaching out and ripping my hair out. Really, I want to set it on fire, anything but show it to my friends at Griffith Junior High, especially not to George. He won't kiss me for sure after this. He'll probably dump me for one of those cha-cha girls who wear those skin-tight Bubblegum pants.

Again, Mango starts trimming my one good wing until my other ear sticks out. I just watch my wing shrink, my face getting redder. I'm trying hard not to cry, but a tear starts rolling down the side of my nose.

When Mango hands me the little mirror and spins me around so I can see the back of my head, I jump off the chair. I reach for the ten dollars in my back pocket, throw it at Mango and run out of César's Salon, down First Street. I don't stop running, not even to stop for the cars speeding down First Street. One car almost hits me. I don't care. I just want to die and never go to Roosevelt or any other high school for as long as I live. I lock myself in my room and turn on the radio to the beginning of "Blue Monday." When I hear the phone ring, I turn up the music, knowing George is trying to call me. When the ringing stops, I walk into the bathroom and look at myself. Pimply-faced and almost bald, my head looks like it's ready to explode. I go into the kitchen and grab the scissors from one of the drawers and watch my hair fall down into the sink. Little by little, my head feels lighter and lighter. In my room, Duran Duran sings "Girls on Film," while I swear I can hear someone, maybe George, yelling "Hey, Lucy!" I just keep cutting and crying.

Sábado Gigante

His father's hands, compared to his own, looked like corn. Gustavo's hands were soft, the color of a brown paper bag. His hands usually held a pen, not a knife, mop or rags like his father's. His dad, Bernardo, washed dishes and bussed tables at La Fonda restaurant near Downtown LA. Gustavo's hands were softer than his mother's. She worked the sewing machines down in the Garment District. Sometimes, from his office window, he would watch the *mexicanos* who looked like his parents boarding the RTD buses or trudging along, maybe chatting with friends or coworkers after they got off at the bus stop.

Gustavo's hands didn't need to count out the *cuoras*, *daimes* and *nicles* for the bus. When he was in high school, he had a bus pass, not a car. Now, driving his own car, his hands gripped the hard plastic of the steering wheel and the gear shift. And now, he was saving up enough money to buy his parents a car, even though he was just an entry-level office assistant. He had just gotten paid enough to make his car and insurance payments. Maybe he could have gotten up at 4 in the morning to help his mother cook breakfast and roll the burritos for lunch, but he needed to sleep. His mother understood. So did his father, who didn't seem to mind walking his mother early in the morning to the bus stop on Whittier Boulevard while carrying both of their lunch pails.

Sometimes, before his parents left their small house, Gustavo could hear them stepping carefully, quietly, trying not to wake up their working son. Sometimes, he'd help his sister Maritza with breakfast, but he usually didn't. She was the oldest daughter, after all. Maritza was the one chosen to cook breakfast for him, the only boy among two sisters. True, they lived in East LA, not Guadalajara or Chihuahua, but the women still had to take care of the men.

Although she and Alma washed the dishes, did the laundry and mopped the floors, they also went to school. Maritza still obeyed Gustavo, but Alma was the rebel. One time, she refused to clean up his room.

"I'm not pickin' up your dirty underwear," she told him, waving his Fruit of the Looms at the end of a broom handle. Gustavo slapped the broom out of Alma's hands, then slapped her hard, leaving a red imprint on Alma's soft brown cheek. He would sometimes see a similar handprint on his father's cheek when he came home drunk from the billiards hall. Gustavo wondered if the slap had come from his mother or another woman.

At work now, Gustavo inputs data, his soft tap, tap on the keyboard soothes his palm, which still stings. When the cute architects at the firm, the one with the mustache like Tom Selleck, asked him to help with a project, Gustavo was thrilled, even if it meant running copies back and forth between offices, copying and collating pages, suffering paper cuts and ink stains for days. Still, it was better than getting the burns, calluses and patches of dry skin that his mother had on her hands. One time, his mother came home with stitches on the fleshy part of her palm, just below the thumb. Maritza had to miss school to take her to the doctor's office. Gustavo couldn't spare the time, and his father's job never gave him time off. His dad was getting paid below minimum wage under the table. Gustavo had a real job, benefits and all. He strived to let his manager know he was not some lazy Mexican. No way.

One Friday, the cute boss with the mustache asked Gustavo to go out with him and a group of other men from the company for a few drinks. Gustavo's heart beat faster. He would later learn that his boss went by the name of Tristan, like the knight from the famous Tristan and Isolde legend. This was the first time he was asked to join in a group outing. In high school, most of the boys avoided him. He had a few friends in class but hardly ever went to the backyard parties held on weekends.

"No fags allowed!" the guys with the flyers would say as soon as Gustavo reached for one. Those same boys belonged to the Boys from Brazil party crew who "dressed to impress" in their skinny ties, black cardigans and black jeans. Most sprayed their hair into stiff round pompadours and wore thin mustaches clipped close to their upper lips. Gustavo desired them and hated them as well but would never say anything. He would just slip one of their flyers into his backpack.

Gustavo's face would burn at the gay slurs. Every morning in high school, he dug deep into his closet for the jeans and T-shirts he saw other boys wear to avoid detection. Sometimes he wore a polo, but not the nice button-down long-sleeve shirts he preferred. Gustavo did not want to chance giving himself away. That was then. This Friday night, he was giving his whole life away to Tristan, at least for the night at the Studio One disco.

With *Thomas Brothers Guide* open to the West Hollywood map on the passenger seat, Gustavo tracked the snaking traffic through Wilshire Boulevard, Vermont Avenue, the Hollywood freeway and finally off the Santa Monica Boulevard ramp. Studio One was so close to his job, so easy to spot with its two stories and flashing windows. As he walked up to the entrance canopy, the thumping beats of "Blue Monday" pounded through the door to his bones, shaking him awake to the night. Tristan waved Gustavo over. He practically ran up to Tristan, who smiled and embraced him. Gustavo almost kissed him but held back.

"So glad you made it," Tristan whispered, his mustache brushing against Gustavo's burning ears.

Suddenly, there was a blonde muscular man in a red tank top staring at them from the door.

"Got your ID?" Tristan asked.

As they pulled out their driver's licenses, the doorman looked Gustavo up and down and said, "Wetback night was yesterday."

"What?" Gustavo asked, his face flushing.

"Don't listen to him," Tristan said, gently caressing Gustavo's lower back. "Let's dance."

Before he knew it, Gustavo was dancing with Tristan under the strobing lights and lasers. Before he knew it, he was drunk on fuzzy navels and Long Island iced teas and making out on the dance floor.

It was the first time he used a condom. It was also the first time he spent a night away from home. When he woke up next to Tristan that early Saturday morning, he smiled. He knew he had to leave before his parents missed him, before his sisters could snitch on him. As he drove down the brightly lit 101, the sun was barely peeking above the San Gabriel mountains, rosy with the dawning. He sang along with the Howard Jones number playing on the radio to help him stay focused on the road and not on the patrol cars prowling the freeways like hungry cats, especially on the weekends. "What Is Love?" Gustavo sang half seriously. Before he could slip his key into the lock for the metal screen door, his mother opened it. She had waited up for him. The black Singer sewing machine with its treadle stood by the window in the living room, glowing in the milky light of the imitation hurricane lamp.

"Next time, call," his mother said as she let him in. "Are you drunk?"

Gustavo shook his head.

Alma stared at him from the slightly opened door of the bedroom she shared with Maritza. She snorted when he said he wasn't drunk. In his room, his mother had lowered the shade and drawn the curtains, just like she did for her husband on those nights he came home drunk.

⚘⚘

On weekends Bernardo would set up their folding table in the garage to play cards with his friends from La Fonda restaurant and pool hall: Juanito, Nacho and Adolfo. They would huddle around the table Gustavo and his sisters used to play Uno, checkers and shape Play-Doh when they were kids. Bernardo would also set up the portable record player from Gustavo's room so as to play *ranchera* music by his three favorites: José Alfredo Jiménez, Vicente Fernández and Antonio Aguilar.

That Saturday afternoon following the Studio One meet-up, Gustavo waited for Tristan to call him. Gustavo knew it would be a long night when he spotted his father's Carnation Milk crate filled with his favorite Mexican albums beside the card table. All afternoon, his mother busied herself with housework and the piecework from the garment factory, sometimes pausing to watch *Sábado Gigante* on the color TV in the living room. When they were younger, his sisters would spend most of their Saturday afternoons at the Puente

Hills Mall, spritzing perfumes at the cosmetics counter at Robinsons May or eating at the pizza joint in the food court. Afterwards, they would join Gustavo and their mother in his bedroom to watch the disco dancing competitors on *Fiebre*, Mexico's answer to *Dance Fever*, which Gustavo also watched religiously on Friday nights. Inevitably, Maritza would make him dance and imitate the moves they saw on the program.

"*Qué bonito bailan*," his mother would say, while Alma clapped like a flamenco dancer.

"You dance just like Giro," Alma would tell him, referring to *Fiebre*'s host.

Soon, she'd be jumping in between Gustavo and Maritza, dancing in time with their routine. One time, all three siblings danced a routine they had choreographed together for Bernardo and his friends. As they waved their hands and jerked their legs in unison, the men laughed and cheered. Later that night, Bernardo cornered his son in the bathroom.

"*Me la vas a pagar* if you turn out to be a *joto*," Bernardo whispered. Then, with a slicing motion, Bernardo said in a quieter breath, "I'll kill you."

From then on, Gustavo just danced with his sisters in his room, never in front of their father. As he grew into his teens, Gustavo learned to hate those Saturday nights. And as the years wore on, his father grew drunker, louder and angrier. By the time Bernardo's friends would leave, usually at around midnight, Bernardo would be sobbing, his head down on the card table, a can of Coors in his fist. Tonight would be no different.

"*¡Aquí no es mi tierra!*" he'd slur, lamenting being so far from his homeland.

After spending most of the night in the garage, Bernardo would be carried back into the house by Gustavo and his mother. As soon as they got him into bed, his mother would go back to her sewing machine in the living room.

"Amá, go to sleep," Gustavo would whisper above the whirring.

"I'm not sleepy anymore," she'd say as she treadled the sewing machine in the dim light of the hurricane lamp. "I have too much work to do."

While Gustavo lay in his bed nursing a headache, he heard his sisters helping his mother with breakfast. He'd barely slept for about two hours before his mother and sisters started clanging pans, slamming drawers and dragging chairs across the linoleum floor. Chorizo, eggs and potatoes were on the menu, but this morning the usually appetizing smells nauseated him. He wanted something light, like the grapefruit and oatmeal breakfast Tristan had offered to entice him into staying at his apartment that early morning before he had left to return home.

"I have to get home before my dad wakes up," Gustavo told Tristan, and kissed him before he left.

"I'll call you tomorrow," Tristan shouted before Gustavo shut the door behind him.

Gustavo's lips tingled at the memory of Tristan's mustache. Before he knew it, Gustavo had dozed off remembering his first kiss, a real kiss with a man he'd desired from the moment he had seen him walking along the white halls of the architectural firm. When Tristan introduced himself as his supervisor, Gustavo could not even say his name.

"Hello, Gus," Tristan said, shaking his hand firmly.

The moment he said, "Gus," the memory of Maritza singing "Get on the bus Gus," when they'd ride the city bus to downtown popped into his head. She kept singing the phrase over and over until he slapped her across the head when his mother wasn't looking. Maritza tried slapping him back, but he ducked before she slapped the metal pole. He laughed at the memory, then dozed off again.

"Are you awake?" Maritza said, pulling Gustavo from his memories. "Mom needs you to mow the lawn."

Gustavo threw a pillow at her as she slammed the door shut. How could she not see that he was not in the mood to do anything today? He covered his ears with one of the shams his mother had made for him after describing one he saw in the bedding department at Bullocks.

"Amá," Maritza yelled. "Gustavo won't get up."

As he looked up at the ceiling, the room began to spin. He gripped the sides of the bed, trying to make the spinning stop. His stomach was in upheaval. He stumbled out of bed and went to the kitchen.

"About time," Bernardo said with a quick nod.

Maritza rolled her eyes as she tucked another corn tortilla into the folds of the dishtowel set between the two men. Gustavo's face burned. They knew he wasn't alone last night. He quickly backed into the bathroom, lifted the toilet lid and threw up. Alma watched him from the open door, gesturing for Maritza to come over.

"Hungover," Maritza said. "He's just like dad on Sundays."

Gustavo could feel Alma nodding, smirking. He wished he could slap it off her face, but the dry heaves were overwhelming. Soon he felt his father's hands shaking him.

"*Toma, m'ijo*," Bernardo said, his father's cracked fingers offering him a can of 7 Up.

Gustavo rolled the cold wet can on his forehead, relieving some of the throbbing of his head. Little by little, he sipped the sweet bubbly drink, until he burped.

His father laughed. "*Ay, m'ijo*, now you're a real man."

As Bernardo lifted his son up from the toilet, Gustavo could smell his father's muskiness. Tristan carried the same deep scent of sweat and firewood. They all had the same male odor. The women, Maritza, Alma and his mother, smelled of blood and stagnant water. As his father tucked him into bed, Gustavo knew he would be carrying Bernardo into bed later that night. He took another sip of the 7 Up Bernardo had set on his nightstand. After one more burp, Gustavo fell into a deep sleep.

Gustavo woke up later that evening to Vicente Fernández singing "*Volver*." His head no longer ached, but he still felt nauseous. Beside him, there was no more fizz left in the 7 Up. He took another sip.

After softly knocking, his mother stepped in. "*¿Cómo te sientes, m'ijo?*" she asked. "Are you still hungover?"

"Are Papá's friends here?"

"Don't you hear them?" she said, jerking her head toward the garage.

Gustavo sat up and ran his hands through his stiffened hair.

"*Pobrecito*," his mother said, shaking her head as she sat down next to him. She rubbed his stubbly face and smiled. Her calloused hands felt warm yet rough.

"Just like your father," she said.

Suddenly, the phone in the living room rang. It was Tristan, Gustavo knew, but he was too exhausted to run and beat Maritza to answer it. No matter.

"It's for you, Gus!" Maritza said through the door. "It's Tristan."

"Who's that?"

"My friend," Gustavo told his mother as he carefully slipped on his running shorts over his Fruit of the Looms. He walked barefoot toward the living room to pick up the receiver left on the spindly wooden telephone table.

"I missed you today," Tristan whispered.

"Missed you, too."

"Do you want to come out tonight?"

Yes, yes! Gustavo wanted to shout, but just whispered "Yes," afraid his mother was watching him. She understood enough English.

"Same place?" Gustavo asked.

"Let's get some dinner first," Tristan said. "How about La Fonda? Do you know it?"

Gustavo's head and heart pounded so hard he could barely answer. He knew La Fonda and La Fonda knew him. How many times had he been there to celebrate birthdays, baptisms and quinceañeras, including Maritza's? How many *mariachi* singers had he lusted after, especially the trumpet player with his thick black hair? The black pants lined with silver buttons would drive him insane.

"Near MacArthur Park?" Gustavo said, trying to hide his fear and joy from Alma, who was eyeing him as his mother was heading back to her sewing machine.

"I'll see you then," Gustavo said.

"Who are you seeing Gus?" It was Alma who had been listening from the kitchen. She knew.

Gustavo blinked, still gripping the receiver. All at once, his hands felt brittle. His mother looked up but went back to sewing.

"None of your business," Gustavo snapped as he headed into the bathroom to get ready. Even now, his instinct to hide from the servers and *mariachi* band members at the restaurant was kicking in. They had known his father since his bachelor days. They had known "Gustavito" since he was a toddler. Years ago, he had bussed tables alongside his father to earn some extra money to buy his first car. This time, Gustavo would walk in as a client, side by side with Tristan, just like the other couples he had seen enter the restaurant. This time, there would be no hiding.

"Who's Tristan, Gus?" Alma asked, following him into the bathroom and locking the door.

Gustavo's face hardened, his hand flexed open, then closed into a fist and then, slowly, opened again.

"He's my boss."

Alma nodded. She leaned back against the door and crossed her arms, looking him in the eye.

"Is he cute, Gus?"

Tristan's sky-blue eyes popped into his head. Gustavo sat down on the toilet; his eyes lowered. Through the small bathroom window, they could hear Bernardo singing "*Sombras nada más*" along with Javier Solís. It was an old song, debuting the year Gustavo was born, 1965. Like most of the *rancheras*, it was about unrequited love, this time for a blue-eyed girl.

"He's beautiful," he gasped.

"*Y sin embargo tus ojos azules*," Bernardo and his friends warbled. "*Azul que tienen el cielo y el mar.*"

Gustavo's fisted hands pushed into his eyes as tears streamed down his face. Alma took his hands and held them, opening up his fists. Gustavo kept his eyes closed but he could tell Alma was looking straight at him.

"It's okay," she said. "It's okay."

Her arms wrapped around him. Together they listened to Bernardo sing along with his friends, completely drunk and unashamed.

Powder Puff

You can't rush this. Nuh-uh. That's why you get up at four in the morning even if you don't have to be at work until nine, because you never know when you might run into one of your old boyfriends or, worse, one of those old nosey skanks from high school like that cha-cha girl Sonya. So, take your time. Ignore your parents, especially your mother, who's banging on the door like she's gonna crash through it.

"¡Apúrate, Mireya!"

Hurry up, for what? Who knows? Today may be the day Principal Díaz will actually ask you out. Take it easy with the foundation and rub it all the way down to your neck. You want to make sure everybody believes the make-up is your natural skin color.

Since this is the first Monday of the month, you break out the Prescriptives Virtual Youth Foundation in "Smooth Honey." One shake and a tiny brown slug pushes through the little hole, goes right on your sponge wedge—fresh squeezed and better than that first-morning cigarette. And it really blends into your skin. No more pink eraser look. At least nowadays the girls at the counter don't have to pretend that, oh yes, you'll glow just like a pink-peach cover girl once you buy this twenty-dollar jar of beauty sauce.

Of course, you use a sponge wedge, not those little cotton balls Mamá uses. The beige foundation drips over them, instead of staying on long enough to be wiped over her face. But once she wipes it on, it stays on, even when it melts down to her neck. Tía Tonia brings her samples from The Broadway, where she works the Chanel counter and gets the samples or "promotions," as she calls them.

Tía is the rich one in the family. She wears pretty black blouses with the two white backward Cs stitched on them. Her skin always looks smooth like condensed milk, not pink and hard like Mamá's. Tía Tonia wears expensive make-up all the time, not just at home or at parties. Her hands are nice and smooth, with long nails covered in pearly reds, browns or purples. But her eyes . . . if she gets too close, it's scary. She lines her eyes like Elizabeth Taylor's *Cleopatra* and draws her eyebrows real high and thin. Mamá and Daddy say she looks like a real movie star. Daddy likes Tía Tonia a lot and always hugs her or holds her hand. He asks my mother why she doesn't fix herself up like Tía does. Mamá just laughs.

"*Una muñeca*," Daddy says, looking at Tía up and down like his head is broken.

⁓⁓

Once you spread the foundation all evenly, put on the powder. Dust it with a big, clean soft brush. Don't use those velour powder puffs like Mamá. After a couple of weeks, they always get sticky thick with dirt, oil and old powder. She always throws them away because they get so filthy. Ever since the Lancôme girl told you how a brush can "evenly distribute" the powder across the pores and actually make the pressed powder in the compact last longer than if you used puffs, you buy that five-piece set with the ebony handles for a hundred dollars. You usually charge it because it's not payday yet and, even if it is, you still can't afford it because your job as a registrar at Fourth Street Elementary School doesn't pay jack shit. Still, it's a great deal, since you usually pay about forty dollars for the powder, and now it'll last you about six months instead of three. It's like a mini-sacrifice, but Principal Díaz is worth every cent, every grain of powder and every hair on that brush. Not like Daddy. Not like Isaac.

One day, while you watched your mother get ready for Tía's party, Daddy walked in and picked up one of those disgusting powder puffs from the little trash can near the toilet. "*Mira*," he said, pushing it up to your face. "You look just like this piece of shit."

You smelled the beer on his breath. He'd been drinking in the garage since morning.

"*Mira, mira*," he said, holding your chin hard, poking your pimples and your eyebrows.

You didn't say anything. You just bit your cheek real hard so you wouldn't cry.

Mamá came into the room and scolded him, "Leave the girl alone, Alejandro."

But Daddy kept poking you until Mamá said she'd get you to "fix" yourself up.

❦

Next, you line your eyes with good eyeliner. What will it be today? Copper Penny by Estée Lauder or Black Vellura by Borghese? You decide on Copper Penny since it's more of a daytime color than the Vellura. You'll save that one for clubbing with your *comadres*.

You're careful to follow the lash line below the eye, so you don't poke yourself like you did so many times before you got the hang of it. Then you pencil the top lid very slowly, pressing a little harder so there aren't any spaces—you want smooth, solid lines. Mamá always uses liquid eyeliner. When you started, you used that "Big Red" pencil liner from Maybelline, but it got so hard after you first used it, you had to melt it with a match in the girls' bathroom to put it on before class started.

You bought that eyeliner at Thrifty's, half a mile from your house. You took a bus there instead of walking to the Kmart on the corner, because the guy you had a crush on since junior high was a Jehovah and sold *Atalaya* magazines in front of Thrifty's with his father every Saturday. Isaac and his father would be dressed in suits and ties, and they'd stand right near the doors, *Atalayas* pressed to their chests. You'd walk by and say "Hi" to him. The first time, Isaac didn't look at you. He was embarrassed. His father always embarrassed him. One time, he made Isaac sit on a kitchen chair in his front yard and practice the accordion. Every kid on the block stopped playing, watching TV, whatever they were doing, and stood right in front of the yard yelling awful things, like "You look like a fag, Isaac" and "Sounds like my grandma's records."

This one kid, Paul, a real loser, threw his football at Isaac's face. Isaac dropped the accordion and ran to his front door. But it was locked. He kept banging on it, but his parents wouldn't let him in. His father shouted something from the window. You couldn't hear because of all the kids shouting, but as soon as he yelled it, Isaac sat back down and started practicing again. Some of the other kids started throwing rocks, and Isaac just kept playing. You ran back into the house, crying like his father had made you sit in the front yard with him. The first thing you did was lock the bathroom door and pull out one of the drawers. You looked for the Borghese compact with the little crest. When you found it, you powdered every inch of your face. Pat, pat, pat. You made sure you covered every purple pimple on your face with the stuff. Pat, pat, pat. You felt a little better and left the make-up on until Isaac's parents let him in the house.

⋙⋘

Don't overdo the eyeshadow. Do it light and "playful," like the lady at the counter told you. You don't want to scare the kids at school. And you don't want Principal Díaz to think you're desperate, like that Sonya who flirts with any man who'll look at her boobs. She still piles on the cheap make-up an inch thick and wears those V-neck blouses like she did in high school. She still has the biggest boobs you ever saw.

The last time you saw Sonya, it was during Back-to-School registration. When she walked in, you were helping parents out with registering their kindergarteners. The moment you saw that wild curly hair and those boobs, you knew it was her. But you couldn't believe she had a kid with her. She always used to say she never wanted any snotnoses to get in the way of her life. But there she was, standing in line with all the other parents, registering this little girl who looked just like a mini-Sonya.

"Hi Sonya," you said.

Sonya looked at you like she didn't know you. She just nodded her head and started filling out the form you pushed in front of her.

You saw the circles under her eyes, even after she tried to hide them with concealer. You use concealer too but the good kind: Anti-Cernes Quick Cover by Chanel. It's so good you don't even know how to say the first two words.

You remembered the lunch periods in high school when Sonya used to sit with all her cheerleader friends and pull out all those lipstick tubes from her imitation Gucci bag. Sonya's favorite was the gold one with silver, swirly lines: Estēe Lauder, of course.

"Hey, check out this color," she'd say, puckering her lips.

"You look like Nastassja Kinky," one of the other cheer-leaders would say.

They'd all laugh like a bunch of clowns.

She didn't know it, but sometimes you'd watch her from a bathroom stall to see what color she would put on for the next period. One time, she caught you.

"What are you doing, you little perv?" she said. "What are you staring at?"

You came out all cool, pretending like you were just there to piss and leave.

"I'll kick your ass next time you do that," she said as you walked out the door.

You did it again, but not until after she got pregnant. By then, she would just splash her face with water, run her hands through her curly hair and run out to class.

That time you registered her kid, Sonya wore make-up, but it was that cheap stuff, like Cornsilk or Almay, cosmetics you can buy at any supermarket. You could tell she didn't rub the foundation around her neck like she should have to make it look natural. Her face looked like it was missing something. You couldn't figure it out until she kissed her little girl. Yep, she wasn't wearing any lipstick! It was funny, because Mamá always pointed to her when she walked to school in front of our house. Mamá always said that Sonya knew how to make herself up. And when she walked back home from cheer-leading practice, Daddy would be standing out there water-ing the lawn, watching her walk by. His head would swivel almost all the way around his neck. He wouldn't say it out loud, but you could see his lips mouthing, "*Qué muñeca.*"

When you really started getting the knack of make-up, Isaac came around. By your senior year, he was saying "Hi" to you and even kissed you a couple of times. He never walked you home, though, or took you out to dances. He took Sonya. That year, Sonya got Isaac and his baby.

That was five years ago. Oh well. There was a reason you were on the other side of the counter and she wasn't. You wanted to ask her if she married Isaac. Or if he left her for another prettier woman who could make herself up better. Would Isaac have loved you instead? You don't have the big boobs, but you wouldn't have cheated on him, like Sonya did with the DJ at the Spring Fling dance. Deep down, you hoped he had found out. You hoped he punched Sonya, like Daddy punched Mamá when she caught him kissing Tía Tonia in their bedroom.

Then one day, Isaac walked into the office. Just like that. He was carrying a little white fuzzy thing in one hand and a cup of coffee. When he got closer to Sonya's little girl, he crouched down.

"You forgot your kitty, sweetie," he said.

You could feel him smiling. The little girl smiled too and grabbed her kitty and his face. He kissed her. Just like that. Then he got up and kissed Sonya. She smiled like he'd given her a stuffed kitten too.

⚞⚟

After putting on some blush—Clarins' "Mystique"—you can finally put on the lipstick. Last week, you wore the Borghese's "Burnt Sugar," which was a little too shimmery, a little too loud. How about something a little sensuous, yet delicate today? Dr. Díaz still hasn't really noticed you, but he sure checked out Sonya during registration. Just like Daddy, his head was going up and down, up and down. How about Clinique's "Sugared Toffee"? Put on the Underwear for Lips lip primer first. When Dr. Díaz finally sees the quality make-up you use, he'll forget about Sonya and her powder puff face.

You remember how Isaac, before he dumped you and started going around with Sonya, told you how pretty you looked with lipstick (Avon's Creamy Caramel?). It made your lips look sexier, and you kept hoping he'd notice and maybe kiss you again because your mother said, "*El maquillaje es magia.*" And she should know because she and Daddy stayed married for forty years. You never saw her without make-up, ever. You know she slept with it on because when you made the beds in the morning, you found lipstick smeared on her pillow. It's not like she worked in an office or anything. Mamá made springs in this hot little factory way out in Long Beach. Every day, especially in the summer, her eye shadow, eyeliner and mascara melted like the watercolors you painted at school.

Mamá kept little sample compacts hidden away in every single drawer of the house. Whenever you looked for a match or a fork, there was always a mini-compact clattering around the drawer like some old piece of candy. All over the house, you'd find little green, blue and black compacts with gold lettering. Her favorite was the Borghese because it had the little silver crest.

"A sign of royalty," she'd say, "*para una princesa italiana.*"

Then she'd pat-pat the powder on her face until her skin looked like the rubber on your pink eraser. You were not allowed to wear make-up until you were sixteen, but you stole a compact anyway. Back then you thought, maybe Sonya would finally notice you, invite you over to her special table for lunch.

After catching you washing your face with a Neutrogena bar and nothing else, Mamá drags you into her bedroom like a little girl. Instead of spanking you or slapping you, she takes out a box from her dresser.

"A gift," she says, placing the box in your hand.

It's a bottle of Lancôme Effacil eye make-up remover. You hold it, tempted to throw the bottle at her even though you know it cost her about thirty dollars. Just because you live with Mamá and Daddy doesn't mean they can still boss you around. After all, you pay them $300 a month in rent, and you never bring any men over to your room, not that there are any men to bring around. How embarrassing it would be to invite some future boyfriend over, maybe Dr. Díaz, and have your parents object. You can always move out, but you're trying to save up to go back to school, and rents are so high in LA. And what about your monthly trips to the Prescriptives counter, not to mention your stops with the consultants at Chanel, Dior, Borghese, Clarins, Clinique, Estée Lauder and Lancôme? No, it's just not time yet.

Remember when Dr. Díaz stopped by your desk and how your heart started thumping fast? He asked you if you could stay late that night and help with finishing up the registration.

"Of course," you said, your heart like a big, bloody cut because you would get to spend a late night with this man more beautiful than the Christmas promotions of all your favorite cosmetic lines.

"Can you help train someone for me?" he asked, his dark red lips growing larger, swallowing you up into their warm softness.

You nodded, thinking, Baby, I would die for you. Just like that Prince song. And even when he brought in Sonya for you to train, you did not mind because you got to spend more time with this man you love as much as those fresh jars of foundation lining the bottom of your bathroom cabinets.

⋙⋘

Use one of those round cotton pads, the ones that look like little quilts. They absorb all the dirt and grime from the greasiest faces. Make-up remover can even lighten up the brownest of skin, at least that's what Tía Tonia with her condensed-milk skin told you.

You rub and rub but you're still as brown as those clay bowls Mamá uses to serve *pozole* for Daddy. One night, while taking a break from the training, after you saw Dr. Díaz trying to kiss Sonya in the supply room, you rubbed the Effacil so hard into your face, you left little red patches on your skin. Through that door crack you could see them rubbing their faces against each other, like they were animals. How long did you stand there? It was like watching a movie. Before you knew it, they were done and Sonya was patting her hair down and pulling out her Estēe Lauder lipstick tube from her back pocket.

"Nastassja Kinky," you whispered.

And they both looked at you through that crack.

"Bitch," Sonya said.

Dr. Díaz put his arms around her and held her. And you? You went back to your desk, pulled out the brand-new Chanel compact, looked at your face. You kept looking, even after Dr. Díaz and Sonya walked out of the supply room. You didn't look at him when he called your name. You just nodded when he asked you to lock the door before you left.

And so you rub and rub, but your skin's no lighter or whiter than it was before. It never will be, no matter how hard you rub, no matter how many times Dad pokes you. No matter what. *Punto.*

❧ ❧

Today, no, today you can't do it. You can't step into that steaming water. You can't rummage through your jars. You can't even pick out some *pinche* cotton pad. No, today it is not to be. You just feel like that used-up powder puff Daddy shoved into your face that day. You open up your closet. Maybe the jars can work their magic on you just by looking at them. Then you remember that Estēe Lauder lipstick tube bulging through Sonya's back pocket and all you see is liquid skin sitting there, flaking inside the glass.

St. Patrick's Day

In the steel mills of Long Beach, Alejandro would work until midnight, leaving in the early afternoon the cozy East LA bungalow he shared with Dolores and her daughter Jennifer. He worked the swing shift from 3 in the afternoon until midnight. He had to get out of bed very carefully to not wake Dolores up. She usually didn't come home until 4 in the morning, sometimes 5, depending on the night. Mondays she came back earlier, like 1 or 2, but Saturdays and Sundays she came in at 4 am.

Alejandro and Moti would drive down Atlantic Boulevard at 2, right after Dolores made him his chorizo and egg burritos and packed a can of Pepsi. Usually she was too exhausted from her shift at El Yuma bar to get up and see him off, but she always left some burritos wrapped in foil in the refrigerator for him. His thermos would already be filled with *café de la olla*.

Long Beach was a factory town filled with smoke and steam. Along with the shipyards, there were steel mills spewing chemical smoke. There were very few beaches left in Long Beach. The ones near Ocean Boulevard, where all the Filipinos used to live and fish, were lined with tall white hotels and their kidney bean pools. In the distance, tankers delivered their oil to the refineries. The ocean breezes never got to the steel mills where Alejandro worked to cool him down.

On getting out of Moti's car, Moti and Alejandro would put on their thick blue helmets, their steel-toed boots weighing them down as they walked across the parking lot to the drudge that awaited them.

"Didn't Ramón tell you that after working for a year you'd get your union card?" Moti asked Alejandro.

"That's bullshit," Alejandro said and spit on the stairs leading up to the wide concrete passageway where they'd line up to punch their time cards.

As he stepped into the cavernous mill, Alejandro smelled the molten metal and felt the heat. Already thick with sweat, his armpits chafed against his flannel shirt. His face began tingling from the acid pooling in the swinging trough he'd use to pour over the steel.

As it grew darker outside, the pit glowed a brighter orange, smoke and steam rising, veiling the men and machines. Sweat mixed with the acid burning Alejandro's nostrils and eyes, even with the bandana covering his nose and mouth. He steadied the pourer, shifting the handles that took all of his strength to pull and then to hold the long nozzle. Drops of acid sprinkled his arms and cheeks. By the time they broke at 8 for lunch out on the benches by the parking lot, the ocean fog had rolled in, cooling Alejandro down a little. He gulped down the salty night breeze that blew over the mill.

"*¿Tienes un faro?*" Moti asked as they sat down.

Alejandro shook his head as he unwrapped his burrito. "I'm sick of smoke. . . . That's all I can taste sometimes."

Moti walked over to another worker, Ramón, and bummed a cigarette and a light.

They talked for a little.

Alejandro looked up and made out one star twinkling through the smoke and the lights illuminating the parking lot. He breathed in the cold ocean air.

❧

"They don't serve Guinness here," Sister Agony on the Cross lamented as she walked back to the table where her sisters in the order sat, dressed in white, ready to save their parishioners from the hell of Long Beach.

"They're steel workers not yuppies," Sister Mary Margaret said, looking around the crowded bar.

Sister Agony sipped from the insipid beer she was served. She had been transferred from San Francisco to teach at the local Catholic school, where many of the steelworkers' children attended. The Catholic schools were no better than the public ones, maybe worse because they squeezed tuition and the cost of uniforms out of these workers.

"Well, I think we should just open up the gates and let their children in for free," Sister Agony said.

"Oh, Lord," Sister Joan the Baptist retorted. "Can't we just enjoy the eve of St. Patrick's Day without arguing about finances?"

The other nuns giggled. They knew the bar was the last place they should be, but after twenty years in the convents and Catholic schools, they deserved a night out.

Pinches monjitas, Alejandro thought as he watched them play pool. Nothing's sacred anymore. Not even a man's space.

"They should be at church," Alejandro whispered to Moti, who was about to shoot the eight ball into a corner pocket.

"*We* should be at church," Moti said. "*No mames, güey.* Let them have some fun."

Moti sipped his bottle of Budweiser, turned to the circle of nuns and tipped the bottle to them.

"*Los San Patricios*," Moti shouted. "A toast to St. Patrick!"

The nuns raised their beer cans to the men.

Alejandro caught the bitterness of the beer in his mouth and rolled it around, eyeing the women's hands, clean but calloused. How does praying wear out the hands? The bar's salty smoke filled his lungs as he watched a nun chalk her cue, lean in and set it down between her middle and index fingers. She poked the white cue ball hard enough to slam it into the 6-ball that shot into the side pocket.

More men from the steel mill poured in through the doors. Many of them swiveled their heads toward the women, who were obviously enjoying themselves. Alejandro wobbled over to the jukebox and punched in the letters for Juan Gabriel's "*No Tengo Dinero.*"

"They're getting sloshed," one of the men observed.

"Oh, they're there already," Moti laughed. "And it's not even San Patricio's day yet."

"Yeah, tomorrow's St. Patrick's Day," Sister Joan whooped, waving her cue stick until it hit Sister Agony on the Cross on the back of her head.

"*¿Qué traes?*" Alejandro asked Moti, tilting his chin toward the pamphlet in his shirt pocket.

Moti jerked his head down, surprised at the rolled booklet. He pulled it out and looked it over.

"Ramón gave it to me," he said.

"You don't read anything, *güey,*" Alejandro said, snatching it out of Moti's hands.

The pages glowed bright orange in the smokey light. "*Huelga*" in bold letters floated up, hovering over the orange page. Below it, a black eagle rose up from the blazing orange. Alejandro had seen the eagle before on TV and on posters at the Johnson market on Whittier Boulevard before they were torn down by the owner or his employees.

He saw the words "*sueldo*" and "*mínimo*." He finished his can of Schlitz, then ordered another from the woman tending the bar.

The more Alejandro read about the steel companies paying him less than the steel workers earned in the Midwest and the Northeast, the more Schlitz he wanted. The beer rose up into his head until he wanted to crack the pool sticks over his knees, then over his supervisor's head. Suddenly, a finger poked his shoulder, making him whip his head to the side.

"*Mírala, mírala,*" Moti said, flapping his eyebrows, poking his chin toward the nuns, who by this time were sitting on the pool table, arms around each other, singing, drowning out Juan Gabriel.

Alejandro slipped off of his stool, onto his feet and yelled at them to shut up. They didn't stop. One of them grabbed a pool cue and pushed her way to Alejandro, who pulled the stick out of her hand. Moti came between them.

"Let's go, *compa,*" he told Alejandro.

The other nuns jumped off the table. They reminded Alejandro of the white rabbits he would see years ago hopping through the strawberry fields of the Santa María Valley. It was up to the field workers to chase them away, slaughter them if possible. The rabbits sometimes made for a tasty dinner at night.

Even with the fog in his brain, he understood that attacking the nuns meant trouble, and he let Moti drag him to his car and home.

≈⋙

The next day, Alejandro walked Dolores' daughter Jennifer to school. After coming in at 4 am, Alejandro had not bothered to get up and prepare breakfast for Jennifer. He nevertheless was up in time to escort her to St. Alphonsus, proud that he was just barely able to afford the costly tuition. She strode just in front of him in her blue, white and taupe plaid skirt and crisp white blouse. Alejandro adored this little girl who was practically his daughter. Her outfit reminded him of the rich kids back in Guadalajara. He too had wanted to wear a uniform instead of worn-out pants and shirt as he tended cows.

As they walked, Jennifer chattered away like a little bird. "*Mira*," she said, pointing to a butterfly alighting on the rose bushes pushing through a neighbor's fence.

"*¿Qué's eso?*"

"A butterfly," she answered.

"*Una monarca*," Alejandro said, attempting to teach her the specific name.

"*Monarca*," Jennifer said breathlessly, looking back at the rose bushes.

When they reached the school, the mothers with their children milled around the nuns, who stood guard at the entrance gates. The nuns were giving out green paper cut-outs to each mother to pin on their children.

"*¿Qué's esto?*" Alejandro asked as he pinned the shamrock to his daughter's shoulder.

"It's St. Patrick's Day today," the nun said.

He squinted at the words printed on the nun's shamrock: "Sister Joan."

The sister wore a royal blue wimple, a skirt and a short-sleeved blouse to match. Sister Joan looked familiar, but Alejandro doubted she could ever hold a cue stick.

Sister Joan, however, remembered the previous night's encounter. She clenched her fists, pursed her lips.

"*Es un trébol*," the nun said, pointing at the shamrock.

Alejandro repeated the word.

"*Trébol*," Jennifer repeated, smoothing out the green construction paper in the morning sun.

Just then, Jennifer grabbed Alejandro's hand and pulled him to the playground, where the other children were starting to line up for their classes. Some of the older students leaned forward against the chain-link fence, watching the passersby.

Another nun gently pushed Jennifer into the line of children forming at the yellow hopscotch squares. Alejandro watched Dolores' daughter easily blend into the babble of English he sometimes heard on the tiny TV in the kitchen as he changed channels, looking for a sports event. He'd sit at the small table, sipping beer, cigarette smoke trailing into the ceiling and out through the window screen above the sink. Some day he would marry Dolores and they would go back to Mexico. He would be able to afford a nice school for Jennifer and a comfortable home for Dolores. But for now, he'd scrape together the money for Jennifer's discount tuition and second-hand school uniform.

As the nun led the streams of students up the stairs, Jennifer waved goodbye. Alejandro waved and pointed to his watch. Jennifer nodded until she disappeared through the heavy double doors. When he got home, Dolores was still sleeping. As quietly as he could, he slipped into bed with Dolores and slept with her until she woke him up.

"It's time to pick up Jennifer," she said.

He could smell the *longaniza* cooking with the refried beans. Soon Dolores would fill and roll the mixture into four tortillas for dinner and then leave for her job at the bar. She would not return until 4 am. He'd wait up for her.

≈⋅≈

As Alejandro and Jennifer walked home together, she chattered about her teacher and friends. She said the teacher had read to the class, *Clifford the Big Red Dog*.

"*Quiero un perrito*," she said, noticing the neighbor's white chihuahua yapping at her from behind the fence.

"When we get a house, you can have a dog," Alejandro promised.

"But we already got a house," she said.

"We need one with a yard."

Jennifer looked down, thinking, rubbing the paper shamrock pinned to her plaid uniform.

"I'll pray for a house," she said.

"Who will you pray to?"

"*San Patricio*."

"Are you Irish now?" Alejandro asked playfully.

Jennifer looked up at Alejandro with one eye shut. "I'm American."

Alejandro laughed, and for the first time that day he felt hungry.

After they got home and had a snack, Alejandro helped Jennifer with her homework, pointing out letters and words he had learned from work and from watching *Benny Hill*, such as "bird," "man" and "ridiculous." After watching a bit of TV, he put Jennifer to bed and then sat at the kitchen table, unable to sleep.

He looked at his hands: dry, wrinkled and veiny, like an old man's hands. Suddenly, he remembered his father's hands, calloused and buckled from hard labor and arthritis. Alejandro rubbed his fingers and started chewing on the cuticles. On the black and white screen, Benny Hill slapped the back of a little old man's head in quick succession as he pointed to a half-naked woman.

Alejandro thought of slapping Dolores' butt while she cooked dinner or breakfast. Or sometimes, when she sat on him while making love.

"Taking my throne," she would say, smiling before she stared down at him.

In Mexico, they could never live like this, with running water, electric power, food, privacy. But at least he could speak his own language without having to think about every word he said. At least in Guadalajara he could again hear the *mariachis* late at night while eating freshly chopped watermelon with *tamarindo, sal y chile.*

Alejandro's mouth watered at the thought of the sweet fruit covered with salt and tangy tamarind sauce. He walked over to the battered refrigerator and opened it, only to find foil-wrapped burritos, cans of Burgie beer and a plastic pitcher of water. No fruit. A thought occurred to him: his neighbor, Don Ramón, had a grapefruit tree sagging with sweet pink *toronjas.*

Outside, the bright lights of downtown LA lit up the night sky. Still a few stars winked down at him. One star shone brighter than the others. Was it Venus? What had Moti told him?

~·~

"If you cross the picket line, you'll never be union," Moti warned before Alejandro slammed the phone down on its cradle.

"Are you going?" Dolores asked.

Alejandro gulped down the last of his Burgie beer and nodded. He had to catch the 260 bus that would take him straight down Atlantic Boulevard to Long Beach. From there, he'd have to take another bus to Joslyn's Galvanized Steel. Ale-

jandro would see his friends picketing, yelling "*¡Huelga!
¡Huelga!*" Some would look away from him. Others would
look him up and down and, if he was lucky, they'd spit on the
street. If not, they'd spit on him.

Before Alejandro left, he picked up Jennifer's paper shamrock from the kitchen table. Its three rounded petals glowed
green in the spring light. He wished he could take it with him
but knew Jennifer would miss it. Instead, he held it and said
a prayer to St. Patrick.

Act of Faith

Once you're married by the Catholic Church, you're married for life.

"*Dicho y hecho*, and that's that," Grandma Fina used to say.

Angelina's husband wanted a divorce so he could be with that *puta* Claudia Mercado. Angelina decided he had to die. That was the only way.

Of course, Frank, Marta and everybody would put up a big stink about it. So what if Father Jorge wouldn't bless or sanctify it. Angelina had had enough of the priest's stupid rules. To conduct a funeral for Antonio would clear the way for her. The way to where, she didn't know, but at least Antonio would be dead.

Angelina finished chopping the garlic and checked on the walnuts boiling in the pan. Almost done. Oooh, maybe she should play some Lola Beltrán, or maybe Linda Ronstadt, so the food can be happy? She put on one of the old scratchy albums Antonio had left her.

"*Aaaaay que lau-re-les tan ver-des*," Lola belted out.

Next, she started shredding the flank steak. The hot meat made her fingers feel tingly, like they had been asleep a long time. She imagined shredding Antonio's face, heart and then his *pito*. She popped a piece of steak into her mouth. How would Claudia like that? Too bad Frank wouldn't participate, but he was a big shot college student now, too good for anything. He probably thought she was as ignorant as her Grandma Fina, who up to her dying day would walk around with coffee grounds stuffed in her socks to cure her sore throats and her coughing. What *m'ijo* doesn't know about women and marriage could fill up this house. Better he didn't know about his father's girlfriends, though, and God knows how many kids. She quickly crossed herself and started roasting the poblano chiles. Next she chopped up the apples, pears and tomatoes.

Frank had vacuumed the living room before he left for classes. He told her he'd be going home with his father for the weekend.

"Fine," Angelina said. "Take your father's side."

Frank picked up his bulging duffle bag and kissed her goodbye.

Just after he left, the phone rang. It was Marta.

"Don't tell me you're not coming," Angelina said.

"I told you, I'd go," Marta said. "But I still think you're crazy. Don't you think what you're doing is sacrilegious . . . *brujería?*"

"No," Angelina said, then she crossed herself.

"Well, Doña Goya and all those little old ladies that follow her think the devil is making you do this. '*Cruz en pecho, diablo en el hecho,*' they say."

"Oh, what do those old hags know? *¡Viejas metiches!*"

Doña Goya had been Grandma Fina's oldest friend, always wearing a black veil and black hose and always rubbing her rosary, praying real loud just before Father Jorge began morning Mass.

"I think they're gonna come to your house and pray for you."

"Pray for me?"

"I told you," Marta said, sounding really tired, ". . . they think your funeral idea is *pura brujería*. That you're putting a curse on your husband."

"But Hermana Tonia is doing the ceremony. Doña Goya goes to her *botica* all the time for a treatment with herbs."

"I guess she thinks only a priest should be doing a funeral."

"Virgen de la Purísima," Angelina said. "You think they're right, don't you?"

Marta just stood there, stuttering.

Angelina knew she'd feel better after the funeral. She'd be able to look out her kitchen window and not have to close the curtains every morning so as not to see Claudia's house sitting right there across the street. Once the funeral was over, she wouldn't have to pull out the bottle of Presidente Brandy she and Antonio used to drink on their anniversary, Frank's birthday and other celebrations.

Angelina crossed herself and promised God this would be the last time she took over one of the church's ceremonies.

"I'll be there," Marta finally said. "How many *panes de muerto* do you need?"

"Bring ten loaves. Antonio was always a big eater."

⋙ ⋘

The coffin knocked around the bed of Angelina's pickup truck as she flew around corners and zipped up the steep hills of Boyle Heights, not really caring if the truck bottom scraped the street. She liked to think she was banging Antonio around, his bones cracking with each slam.

"*¡Ay que laureles tan verdes!*" Angelina belted out with Lola Beltrán. Her veil flapped with the speed of the truck while her rosary swung over the rearview mirror with each swerve around corners. Rudy gripped the door handle with both hands.

"Don't worry, *m'ijo*," Angelina said, "I just wanna shake Antonio up a little bit."

When they got to Angelina's house, Rudy threw up into the rose bushes.

She laughed and said, "Rudy, you're more of an old lady than I am."

Angelina opened the truck's tailgate and grabbed the coffin, pulled on it until Rudy wiped his face and then grabbed the side of the coffin. Unsteadily, they carried it to the foot of the stairs.

Rudy looked up the steep stairs and gave a long whistle.

"Don't look at me," Angelina said. "Antonio wanted 'the house on the hill' like he was some kind of *pinche rico* or king."

As they inched up the cement steps, Angelina noticed the nicks on the purple paint Rudy had applied to the pine box. So what, she thought. Like Antonio deserved a nice, new shiny coffin. He's lucky he's even got one. She should just throw his bones straight into the fire. But she couldn't do that to Frank. She had to keep the funeral somewhat respectful, even if her son wouldn't be there. If anything, Rudy's artwork deserved some respect, and he was Frank's best friend. Antonio's skeleton, even the skull, was a piece of art, like something she'd seen in one of those funny little stores Frank would take her to with all these crazy pictures costing like $500, even though they looked like your own kid could make them in kindergarten.

They hauled the coffin up the stairs, panting and walking very slowly. Angelina tried not to trip over her long red skirt. What if she fell? she thought. The image of Antonio's purple coffin laying on top of her body made her go a little slower. Rudy just kept on lugging the thing. Thank God he was there to help her. Frank would never do this.

When she told him about the funeral, he shook his head and said, "Mom, you're creeping me out."

Creeping him out, her ass! He was creeped out by a funeral for his father, but he wasn't creeped out when he visited Antonio and his little girlfriend across the street, was he? No, that was no problem, but when his own mother asked him to help burn the coffin with the skeleton, clothes and all, now that was a problem. Angelina got so worked up, she started pushing Rudy harder.

"Take it easy, will ya?"

When they got the coffin to the porch, Angelina told Rudy to take a break.

"Where do you want this thing?"

"In the living room," she said. "We're gonna lay him out and get him ready for the wake tonight."

She noticed him looking at her wall covered with saints, sacred hearts and La Virgen de Guadalupe.

"You sure have a lotta saints here. Didn't you use to have family photos up there?"

"Yeah, but that was a while ago."

"Where'd you put them?"

"In a box somewhere."

Rudy saw her bride picture: she was standing by herself in front of a little waterfall at La Encantada Park.

"How old were you when you got married?"

"Oooh, *m'ijo*, I was seventeen . . . no eighteen."

"Wow."

"*Qué* 'wow' *ni que nada*. It's not like I'm a hundred years old now."

Rudy looked at her and then went up to a picture of Frank. "Frank looks like you."

"Thank God."

They placed the coffin on the two sawhorses she'd just bought that morning at the Home Depot. She had draped a rainbow-colored cotton blanket over them. Behind the coffin, on the now-empty entertainment center, she had placed dozens of multicolored votive candles. As Rudy helped her light them, Angelina wondered why he wasn't "creeped out." Of course, she had paid him $100 for the coffin and skeleton, although she thought that was too expensive. Anyway, she had been friends with his mother, Jenny Ortega, former cha-cha girl and the 1983 Tower Queen for Griffith High School. She'd been a bitch, but her son was a true gentleman. Very handsome too, but of course, his father was white. Too bad he came out *prieto* like his mother.

⸻

Angelina, Hermana Tonia and Rudy assembled solemnly for the funeral. Marta had stopped by long enough to drop off the *panes de muerto,* but as soon as she saw the coffin and Hermana Tonia, she took off fast.

Hermana Tonia started reciting the funeral rites from the *Order of Christian Funerals.* The living room was wall-to-wall roses. Angelina had used the last of the money she had gotten from the sale of Grandma Fina's house to buy them. In the candlelight, the roses' shadows bobbed up and down like dozens of mourners. The candlelight shone on the coffin that Rudy had painted. The Virgen de Guadalupe he had drawn on the coffin lid was just like the picture she had hanging on her living room wall.

Dressed in her black *rebozo* and white tunic and pants, Hermana Tonia looked like one of those Indian women with the red dot on their foreheads. Tonia spoke in a low, dry voice about God's mercy for the souls of the dead. Next, she sprinkled holy water from an abalone shell. When she began the *Padre Nuestro*, suddenly Doña Goya and the rest of her cronies could be heard praying outside the front door.

"*¿Qué es eso?*" Hermana Tonia asked.

"It's only Doña Goya," Angelina said.

"Get rid of her. I can't do this if they're making that racket."

Angelina opened the door and told the old ladies to leave. But they kept on praying their fifth recitation of the "Act of Faith." Angelina ran around the corner of the house and came back dragging a gushing hose. They finally stopped and looked at her.

"Angelita," Doña Goya said, "it's a sin what you're doing."

"It's my business if I wanna hold a funeral."

Doña Goya started crying. "Your Grandma Fina . . ."

"Don't you dare bring Grandma Fina into this," Angelina warned. "I'm not gonna feel bad about this, just like Antonio doesn't feel bad about jack."

"But this curse, *hija* . . ."

"Shut up. You don't even know what I'm doing."

"*¿Qué pasó?* You're acting like you weren't even raised by a decent woman like Josefina."

"I'm acting like I wanna act, and I'm not gonna let a bunch of old ladies who haven't had sex with anybody for forty years tell me how to live my life."

The *viejitas* started whispering really fast to each other, shaking their heads.

"Don't shake your heads at me, like you're some kinda saints. I know 'bout you, and you and you. And I know 'bout your kids too."

With that, they turned and started walking down the steps, slowly at first and then taking little hops like fat, black rabbits.

❧ ❧

After the funeral, Angelina served up *chiles en nogada* in the kitchen. She kept the window open and would peek out as she passed by. Claudia's house was dark. Where could they be? What did she care anyway?

"*¿Otro chile?*" Angelina asked Hermana Tonia.

"*Ay, sí.* They're delicious," she said, accepting her sixth stuffed poblano pepper.

"And you, Rudy?"

"I'll take two more," he said.

"Good! You should take some to your mother."

Angelina scooped out the last of the chiles into a Tupperware bowl. "Tell your mother I'm sorry I took up so much of your time."

"She doesn't care."

"You sound like Frank. Of course, we care."

In the living room, the candles flickered in the dark. The twilight was giving way to the night, but Angelina felt energized as if the day was just beginning. Lola Beltrán sang "*Paloma negra*," scratchy but strong from the console. Angelina poured out another shot of brandy and stood up.

"A toast to Antonio's death!"

After toasting his death, they toasted to the funeral and to Rudy for his artwork.

"What did you say Antonio was made out of?" Hermana Tonia asked.

"Papier-mâché," Rudy said.

"Then it should burn real easy," she said, sipping from her glass.

Rudy and Angelina looked at each other.

"I don't wanna burn it," Angelina said. "I wanna keep it right here in the living room."

"No," Hermana Tonia said, "you have to burn it if you want the funeral to be complete. You can keep the ashes. Keep them in a bowl or throw them in Claudia's front yard, but don't keep the coffin or the skeleton as it is."

"*¿Por qué no?*" Angelina said, thinking that Hermana Tonia was just like Doña Goya.

"Because then you're making fun of God, not just Antonio."

"I'm not making fun of anybody."

Somebody started banging on the door. Rudy opened it, and Antonio walked in and up to the coffin.

"So this is it, huh?" Antonio said. "What kind of *brujería* is this?"

"Get out of here, you, you *hijo de la chingada*," Angelina said, running over to the coffin. "This isn't your house anymore. Go back to your little whore and marry her."

Antonio reached past her and pushed the coffin over, dumping the skeleton.

"*¡Pinche bruja!*" he shouted in Angelina's face.

Rudy pushed Antonio.

"And you . . ." Antonio said, pushing Rudy back and over the coffin. Then he picked up the skeleton and waved it in front of Rudy's face. "Is this supposed to be me?"

"Leave him alone! I'm calling the police," Angelina yelled.

Hermana Tonia approached, her arms heavy with a *molcajete*, ready to smash it over Antonio's head.

Antonio walked out the front door, laughing. "*¡Brujas!*" he shouted. "I'm still alive, and I'm not gonna die."

They watched him as he hopped down the stairs and crossed the street back to Claudia's house. Through the kitchen window, they could see Claudia waiting in her nightie. As soon as Antonio walked in, he turned off the lights.

⸙⸙

The next day, Rudy showed up with his truck. After hauling the coffin down the hill, Angelina gratefully climbed into the cab. She turned up Cuco Sánchez on the radio so she could hear it over the pickup's engine. The smoke from Rudy's cigarettes tickled her throat as she tried to belt out "*La cama de piedra.*" In the setting sun, the San Bernardino Mountains glowed pink and purple.

"Where are we going?" he asked.

"Far," Angelina said.

When they got to Joshua State Park, Angelina drove down the road for a mile or two before parking near a deserted campfire.

"We're here," Angelina said. She jumped out of the truck and straightened out her skirt.

"Now what?"

"Let's get the coffin."

Rudy shook his head, tossed his cigarette and stubbed it out with his shoe. "After all that work I put into it?" he said.

"I paid you for it, didn't I?"

Rudy sat down and lit another cigarette.

"Why do you think I brought you out here?" Angelina said.

He shrugged and pretended to look at the Joshua trees. Why the fuck had she brought him here? The brandy was getting her soused. Maybe she wanted to fuck. She's drunk enough Presidente to help her do just about anything. It almost feels like love. Why not make love? But not now. First there's some burning to do.

"Well, if you won't do it . . ." Angelina said as she walked up to the back of the truck, her feet kicking up dust. She pulled at the coffin so hard it fell to the ground.

"It's your money," Rudy said as he helped her lay the coffin over the dead campfire.

"Too bad Grandma Fina's not here. She liked all this fire and ceremony stuff," she said. "I think this is why she was into the Catholic Church."

Angelina poured brandy over the skeleton, while Rudy set the skull on fire. It took about an hour for everything to burn. With the Santa Ana winds blowing, all the ashes blew into the Joshua forest.

"Can we just stay here for a little while?" Angelina said.

Rudy shrugged his shoulders and climbed into the truck's cab. Angelina climbed into the other side and turned on the radio. María de Lourdes sang "*Tú, Solo Tú*." Angelina hummed along with it, then started singing.

Rudy smiled at her and laughed a little. "You're sooo blasted," he said.

"So what?" she said. "I'm a free woman. I can do whatever the hell I want. *Túúúúú solo túúúúúú.*"

"Are we gonna spend the whole night here?"

"I just don't wanna go back yet. What for?"

Rudy lit a cigarette for her. In the sky, she could see so many stars and wondered if Grandma Fina was looking down at her.

"Grandma Fina's probably getting a place in hell ready for me."

"No, she isn't."

Before she knew it, Angelina was crying so hard she started choking on the cigarette smoke. "She's probably saying, 'That sinning whore's no granddaughter of mine. I didn't raise a heretic.'"

Angelina wiped her eyes and nose with her skirt. So what if Rudy saw her leg, her old wrinkly thighs with their spider veins. What did he care? He was just a boy starting his life. Just a boy with all the young girls waiting for him. Someday, he'd fall in love and get married. Someday, he'd dump his old ugly wife for a new woman. Just like Antonio.

"Don't ever get married, Rudy."

He almost choked on his cigarette smoke.

"I think we better go," she said, starting the engine.

"Not yet. You're not ready."

"You're not my husband."

"I know. He's dead."

Angelina couldn't make his face out in the shadow of the truck. She turned off the engine and pulled a blanket from behind the seat. Rudy smiled at her like Frank used to when he was little as she tucked him into bed. Outside, the Santa Ana winds whistled through the cracks in the windows.

❧ ❧

In the morning they drove back, her head pounding with *ranchera* music on the radio. Angelina felt dry and dusty, like an old empty bottle. Rudy wasn't able to sleep, though Angelina told him she was all right. In the sunlight, with his little mustache and beard, he looked like Juan Diego seeing the

Virgen de Guadalupe floating in front of him, his *tilma* filled with roses.

When Angelina dropped Rudy off at his house, she felt cold. She grew colder as she drove back to her own house, thinking about climbing up the steps just to end up in an old hollow space. She started up the truck again and drove back to Rudy's place. His dog Peewee started barking at her as she walked around to the garage where he lived. She just hoped that Jenny didn't come out to greet her. *Qué vergüenza*. Here she was, a grown woman visiting some twenty-something kid because she was lonely. For a moment, she had second thoughts, but the thought of those stairs made her keep walking to the garage.

"Rudy, Rudy," she whispered through the screened window.

She could make out his dark shadow getting up from the bed. The smell of brandy got stronger as his steps came closer.

"Angelina, what's wrong?"

"Can we talk a little?"

Angelina walked straight into his bedroom and sat down on his narrow bed. It smelled like Tide. His mother must have just changed the sheets that day. Paint tubes and brushes lay on the floor, partly painted canvases leaned against a wall. Rudy dragged his chair out hard and sat right down next to her.

"Why can't you go home? Aren't you tired?"

"No. Antonio's still alive."

Rudy lit a cigarette.

"According to the Church, Antonio's still my husband."

"According to you, he's dead. We did that little ceremony, remember?"

She had killed Antonio just like he had killed her the moment he started cheating on her. And he had kept on killing her.

"Do you wanna sleep here?" Rudy asked.

Angelina choked on her saliva so hard, she didn't even notice that she laid herself down or that Rudy had taken off her shoes. She got up for a moment and took off her dress, then got back in bed in her bra and panties. Rudy laid down next to her.

"You won't believe this," she said. "Antonio's the only guy I ever slept with in my whole life."

"I believe it," Rudy said.

Little Soldiers

———

"**H**old still."

Martín tugged at his grandson's ponytail as if he could control its length. Under the fluorescent lighting, Beto's hair glowed yellow, not gold like his father's. Martín rolled Beto's head around, pulling on the hair that reached down to the middle of Beto's back. He eyed the blonde strands like a sniper eyes a target. But instead of a rifle, Martín would use his handy spray bottle, shears and pomade to keep Beto's unruly hair down.

Lalo, Martín's *compadre* and cousin, sat reading *La Opinión* newspaper and eating a *tortuguita* Beto's mother had brought home from El Gallo bakery. Sandra had bought a whole plate of Mexican sweet breads that morning, and they were nearly all gone. Lalo, Martín, Rudolfo and Ezequiel had all attacked the platter of *pan dulce* before she could even set it down.

"Didn't that *pleito* at your neighbor's house teach you anything?" Rudolfo yelled at Ezekiel, who was munching on a *cochinito*.

"He messed one too many times with my Chivas," Ezekiel said. "So I popped him."

"You're getting too old to fight," Rudolfo mumbled.

"You're too old," Ezekiel said, rearing up behind Rudolfo. "Men never stop fighting."

"*Cálmate, compa,*" Martín said as he reached for his spray bottle. "Las Chivas are gonna win, anyway."

Rudolfo shook his head. "That pinche Guadalajara team."

"Who cares?" Lalo said from behind his newspaper.

"Hey, we know who rules the field," Ezekiel said and then popped the last bit of the piggy-shaped pastry into his mouth.

"Club Atlas, *cabrón,*" Lalo said, snapping his paper.

"What do you think, Beto?" Martín asked as he cut through the rubber band and combed through Beto's hair.

"Don't call me that," Beto said. "Call me Robert."

"*Uy, uy, uy, qué* touchy!" countered Martín, then looked at his grandson's face in the mirror.

Beto's green eyes blazed at him.

Martín looked away. Just like his mother, Martín thought. Sandra needs to teach him better manners . . . as if she had them herself! He pulled at the cape just below his grandson's neck, tugging it so that Beto's head jerked back a little. Then, he brought out his sharpest shears that would cut through Beto's ponytail with one snip, no sticking. Only the best equipment in his shop. God knows, he'd worked hard enough after serving this thankless country in Korea. And what for? So he could lose one eye and come back and have to repeatedly register with the Migra? Shit, the Army didn't even have the decency to get him the bank loan he needed to pay for his shop. None of his discharge papers convinced the bank he'd pay the money back, not as the loan officer stared at his big, brown Mexican face.

"You're considered a risk," the bank manager had told him.

Martín narrowed his eyes. He sat up straight and took a deep breath. As he exhaled, his hands gripped his knees.

"But I was a sergeant in the Army," Martín told him. "I have the papers."

And just as Martín was about to pull out the papers from his back pocket, the bank manager, one of those college big-shot "Chicanos," stood up and shook his hand.

"I'm sorry, *compa*," he said, "but you just got out of the Army and you don't have the necessary collateral to cover the loan."

Puro pedo. He had a house, thanks to the GI bill but now this *pendejo* was denying him the money he needed to pay off the mortgage. Martín looked at the manager's hand, held out for him to shake. He wasn't shaking shit. In the end, he walked out. In the end, it was his wife Viviana's family who came through with the money for the down payment.

"Look," he said, holding up the long strands of the clipped ponytail as if they were an infected part of Beto's body.

Beto rolled his eyes.

Martín put the hair in a plastic bag for Sandra as a souvenir or as kindling to burn to make sure no one cast some curse on her son. Martín laughed to himself.

"What's so funny?" Beto asked.

Martín laughed again, so he could hear it echo off the tiled floor. "*Ay, m'ijo*, you're going to look so good."

Most of his *compadres* would be over later for dominoes, and he didn't want to have to explain why his daughter kept him from raising his grandson like a man instead of a pampered gringo hood. It was too strange. Sandra had always been the good daughter, obedient, polite. As a teenager, she wasn't boy-crazy like her sister Marisol, or just stupid like her brother Daniel. Sandra had gone to college . . . and that's when she met that *desgraciado* Eddie Bannister, who convinced her to move in with him, despite what her parents said. Martín almost spat when he thought about that kid. But that *cabrón* did give him a grandson, even if he was an ungrateful half-gringo.

"Are you done yet?" Beto asked as he tried pulling the cape off.

"Hold on. I'm gonna make you look like your grandpa when he was young."

With his Cobalt shears, Martín pointed to a framed picture of himself smiling in his Army uniform with big brass buttons on the lapels and corporal chevrons.

"That's you?" Beto asked.

"Yeah."

"Army's full of shit."

Martín's hand stopped cutting. Lalo, Ezekiel and Rudolfo turned to them. That's exactly what Martín had thought when he was drafted, and he often thought the same thing throughout his tour. But when Beto said it, he felt like digging those shears into his skull.

"You wanna know what's bullshit? Here, this is what's bullshit," he said, pulling his glass eye right out of his socket and pushing it right up to his grandson's face.

Beto's head jerked, and he shrunk down into the barber's chair.

"Talk to me about bullshit when you've lost your eye fighting the Commies."

❧❧

Snip, snip, snip. Martín continued cutting Beto's hair. Would he tell Sandra about shoving the eye into her son's face? If he did, would Sandra go away again?

Martín brought out the flat topper from the drawer, to Beto's dismay. Martín remembered his own father threatening to scalp him if he ever let his hair grow past the tips of his ears.

"Mom said you were just going to cut off the ponytail," Beto said.

"When the bishop calls you a soldier for the church, you're gonna look like one."

Beto rolled his eyes, and Martín conked him on the head with the butt of the clippers.

"I'm not your mother," Martín said.

Beto started breathing heavily.

Martín wanted to conk him again but he didn't trust Beto to keep his mouth shut about the clippers or the eyeball. Instead, he brought out his comb, ran it through his grandson's hair and started trimming some more. The shears felt a little heavier than usual because of his arthritis. He had been feeling this pain for years now, ever since Viviana died. *Ni modo.* He had a daughter and grandson to support now.

"Can we listen to the radio?" Beto asked.

"Okay. But none of that rap *mugrero.*"

When his grandson hopped out of the chair to put the radio on, Martín noticed how Beto's head was almost level with his own six-foot stature. In the mirror, Martín saw Beto's dark eyes look at him like a stranger. Did Beto think he was better because he was half *gabacho*?

The first day Sandra and Beto moved in, Beto looked straight at Martín, not showing any respect. Goddammit, Beto reminded him more and more of those white boys he had confronted at Roosevelt High School when he was Beto's age. There were only about fifty of them in the whole school but they acted like they owned the place. The teachers always gave them the best grades, and some of them were the only ones who went to college. If only his teachers could look at him now, a businessman with money in the bank and kids with college degrees.

"I'm only doing this for Mom," Beto said as he got back into the chair.

"I know."

Martín came close to slicing off the top of Beto's ear, and his heart started beating faster. Instead of kicking the barber chair, he gripped the shears and slowly cut closer to Beto's scalp. The clippers had just started humming in his hand, when Sandra walked in with some coffee and *pan dulce*. Martín turned off the clippers.

"*Buenos días, señores,*" she said.

In her ruffled high-neck blouse and plaid skirt, Sandra still looked like the same girl who attended Sacred Heart of Mary. She was even wearing the lipstick Martín had told her to wear to her teaching job at Roosevelt.

Sandra greeted Lalo, Martín, Rudolfo and Ezequiel. They looked up eagerly and held out their hands to touch hers and to grab a piece of sweet bread.

"*Comelones*, leave me a piece," Martín warned as he reached into the bag Sandra had brought and pulled out a *cochinito*, then took a sip of coffee.

Sandra walked right up to Beto and held his face in her hands. With their freshly painted pink nails, she stroked Beto's shorn golden hair. And then she kissed him on the cheek.

As for Martín, she just stared at him in disapproval.

"I thought you said he was only gonna cut my ponytail," Beto complained as he also gave Martín a resentful look.

"I'm sorry," Sandra said, "but it's just for today."

When she tried to kiss him again, he turned his head.

"You can grow your hair back as long as you like after today."

"Not in my house," Martín said.

"You cut too much," Sandra said in her cry-baby voice.

"You stick to teaching. I'm the barber in the family."

"Believe me," Sandra said as she turned to glare at him, "I know."

"At least," Martín said as he wiped the blades of the scissors, "I'm working."

Again, Sandra shot him a hateful look.

Martín thought she was about to leave, but instead she went to the radio and turned it up. A female group was singing "He Was Really Sayin' Somethin'." Martín hadn't heard that one in a while. It took him back to 1966, when Sandra and her sister Marisol would sweep up the hair on the floor while they sang that crazy music of theirs.

He turned on the clippers again. Beto said something, but Martín couldn't hear him.

"What?" Martín shouted over the buzzing.

"Mom's going back to college, she's getting a masters."

"I know. I'm paying for it, remember?"

The buzzing blades cut through the soft hair, leaving less and less on the sides of his head.

"She'll be a principal, and then we'll leave," Beto yelled.

So what? Martín thought. Let her leave. They'll both come back after the next guy leaves her. Martín wondered if Sandra meant to sit in Eddie's old chair, where he trained and worked before he left. For five years, Eddie worked at the barbershop and then left to follow Sandra up to Santa Cruz to work at some men's salon. What real man works at a hair salon instead of a barbershop? he thought. After all that training, it went to waste after he got killed in Vietnam, without marrying *m'ija* and leaving me with a bastard grandson.

"Ouch!" Beto said, yanking his head away from Martín's hands.

"Will you be careful?!" Sandra scolded and then jumped up to check Beto's head.

Again, she kissed him. Without looking up at Martín, she went back to Eddie's chair to read her magazine. Martín hadn't replaced that chair in thirty years, not that he didn't get offers. Every day, all these yuppie Chicanos kept asking how much he wanted for that beat-up chair that was part of the shop's identity.

When Martín first started training Eddie, he was just a kid, maybe fifteen at most. Viviana was always watching out for the neighborhood youths.

"What are you bringing me now?" Martín asked, looking up at this snotnose with a tall skinny body and hair like a broom who reminded him of those Roosevelt *gabachos*.

"He's a foster child, Martín," Viviana said.

"Well, get me a Mexican one. This guy's already gonna get enough chances."

At that, Eddie grabbed a broom and started sweeping. Martín watched him for a while, settling into a barber chair, as Eddie swept deep into the corners. After he finished, he grabbed the mop left in the corner by Sandra, who had not finished mopping before leaving for school.

"I guess he can help me," Martín said, rubbing his eyes.

How did Viviana know that stupid kid would worm his way into the barbershop? In time, Martín learned to respect Eddie's sharp eye for the latest haircuts. He was still going to school, where he noticed all those drugged-up kids' latest styles. When they started growing out their hair like the girls, Martín thought that was the end of barbershops. But with Eddie's help, he survived. Those *locos* who wanted Beatles hair had to go somewhere but were still too macho for a hair salon. And when Eddie told him about that Afro style, he learned how to do that, too, even when his *compadres* made fun of him. They stopped laughing, though, once he paid off the shop and his house.

When Eddie graduated from high school, Martín figured Eddie would look for a better job.

"No sir," he said all humble and respectful. "I'm staying."

"As soon as I get Sandra off to college," Martín told him, "I'll give you a raise."

It was only fair, Martín thought. But then Eddie and Sandra came home one afternoon and told him they were both going to UC Santa Cruz. Martín almost pulled the money for the school.

"Let them go," Viviana told him.

By that time, the cancer was catching up with her, making her more sentimental about love and life. Otherwise, Martín knew she would have taken his side.

"But he tricked me," Martín grumbled.

"And you got five cheap years of labor out of him."

⚞ ⚞

He could see the white of Beto's scalp underneath the short stiff hairs. With his trimmers, he evened out the hair length and stood back. Beto's head seemed so small now without all that wild hair. More like an eight- than a twelve-year-old.

"Are you done?" Sandra asked.

"Almost."

Martín opened his little tin of pomade and slowly worked it into his grandson's hair and scalp. It was the first time he had touched him with his own hands since he came to live there. He finished and pulled the cape off his grandson.

"Hold it," he ordered abruptly.

From one of the many little drawers, Martín took out a big soft brush and swished it over Beto's neck, trying to sweep off as many small pieces of hair as he could. He tried to get every little stiff hair that would show up on his grandson's white shirt and suit.

"Can I go now?" Beto asked, looking at Sandra.

She nodded.

They could hear the door slam as Beto ran out of the barbershop to Martín's house. Sandra looked down and gently caressed the mutilated ponytail in the plastic bag.

"You didn't have to cut it all," she lamented to her father.

Martín wiped his shears with a clean white cloth and placed them in a glass full of Barbicide. He then grabbed the clippers and released the blades onto the fabric.

Sandra sighed. "This is why I didn't want to come back."

Martín snapped the cape hard. "What?" he asked as he wiped it down with disinfectant.

"I'm thirty-two years old and I deserve some respect."

It didn't matter that the hairstyle suited Beto's small features and that he finally looked like a real man. Couldn't Sandra see that?

"If you had wanted respect, you would've told your parents about Eddie and Beto. No secrets."

"Papá, that was twelve years ago."

Martín shook his head.

"I got my college degree. I'm studying for my master's. What's it gonna take?"

Shrugging his shoulders, Martín shut off the radio and walked over to turn off the lights.

"We better get Beto ready," Martín said.

Sandra threw the ponytail into the trash and walked out the door.

From the backseat of the car, Martín could see that Beto's neck looked neat and clean, ready for that march down the aisle to the bishop and his blessing. Yes, he'd done a clean job, but Sandra wouldn't even speak to him. Wouldn't even look at him. Martín fumed.

Is this what they taught kids at college? he thought. How to be disrespectful and rude to your parents, the ones who loved you and supported you through everything.

"You know your grandmother would have been proud," Martín said.

Sandra turned up the radio. Martín rubbed the back of his neck and gripped his chin. So why did they come back if they were going to treat him like a dog, he wondered. He clenched and unclenched his jaw as Sandra parked the car in front of St. Alphonsus.

"Go ahead, *m'ijo*," she said. "I'll meet you inside."

¿M'ijo? . . . What a candy-ass, Martín thought. He was about to open his door when he felt Sandra grab his arm.

"Look, just because we're living with you doesn't mean you can treat us like we're your little servants," Sandra said. "Those days are over."

"I'm not treating you like a servant," he said, feeling the heat in the car. "You're my daughter. You have a duty . . ."

"Shhh!" Sandra shook her head and pressed her finger against her lips.

"You're crazy," Martín said.

He opened the door and lifted himself out of the car. His *compadre* Lalo, with his white cowboy hat and best button-down shirt waited outside the church. Sandra just kept hitting the steering wheel with her hands, squeezing her eyes shut.

She's gonna cry, Martín thought, as she walked beside him. He pushed open the church doors just as he heard her sniffle.

"What's going on?" Lalo asked.

"Nothing, nothing," Martín said, "just *pendejadas* as usual."

About twenty catechism students stood around the church foyer, squeaking across the floor with shiny black patent-leather shoes and chattering. Both men sat down in the front pew so they could see the bishop dressed in his fancy robe and pointed hat.

As soon as an old lady started singing, every single *viejita* in East LA started croaking out *aleluyas*. *Híjole*, Martín thought, didn't they know they sounded like cats in heat? How Viviana had put up with the racket, he never knew. Martín quickly crossed himself and looked at Lalo, who sat with his eyes closed and arms crossed. The boys and girls started marching down the aisle, their hands in prayer position. One-by-one, like he was the big *caca*, the bishop laid his hands on them. He said something about the Holy Ghost making these kids perfect Christians and soldiers of Jesus Christ.

Huh? What did the bishop know about raising kids? Martín scoffed to himself. How about being a soldier? The socket of his missing eye started to itch. In another moment he'd throw his eye at the bishop. Then he quickly crossed himself and whispered "*Perdóname*," and thought of Viviana, how she would be crying and feeling proud of her grandson. *¡Ay, Viviana!*

Then, when all the kids kneeled in front of the altar, the bishop said something about sending the Holy Spirit a pair of cleats. Maybe he didn't hear right. With the little altar boy following him around with a little gold bowl, the bishop dipped his finger in the bowl and made the sign of the cross on each kid's forehead.

"I sign thee with the sign of the cross and confirm thee with the chrism of salvation, in the name of the Father and of the Son and of the Holy Ghost," the bishop recited.

Martín looked around, trying to find his daughter, but the church was packed with old ladies, *compadres, comadres,* everybody! It was like Christmas, which was about the only other time he came to church. He'd find her in front of the church after the ceremony. Maybe she'd cool down by then.

⤞⤝

Sandra and Beto didn't even bother to come back home after the ceremony. Lalo informed Martín that Sandra's friend from high school had taken her and Beto to Shakey's Pizza. Martín sat in his barber chair trying to remember where Sandra had put Beto's ponytail. On the radio, "I'm Your Puppet" warbled through the tinny speaker.

"A man works all of his life to support his family, and this is all that's left," Martín said, then got up to take down his Army picture.

For a moment, he couldn't remember where that picture had been taken. Before he settled back into Eddie's chair, he checked under the old padded bench. He hadn't been on his knees in a long time, not since he knelt by Viviana's bed as she was dying in that hospital. Ah, there it was, he spotted it in the trash can, lying there like a snake.

He picked up the plastic bag, gold strands caught the light.

"What's that?" Lalo asked.

"Beto's hair."

Before Lalo could touch it, Martín shoved it into his pocket.

Lalo walked toward the wooden box and was about to empty it before Martín called out to him.

"Forget it, Lalo. No dominoes tonight."

Martín had to get away from Lalo quickly before he started bawling like a baby. He went to the front door and locked up the shop quickly, turning his back to Lalo. He walked two steps toward the back house, then stopped.

"*Oye*, Lalo . . ."

"Yes, Martín?"

"Where does Sandra's friend live?"

Lalo tilted his head toward the brightly lit boulevard stretching toward downtown.

"It's a good night for a walk, *¿que no?*" Lalo suggested.

Martín was already marching down Whittier Boulevard.

Angry Blood

When the head housekeeper with the red hair and eyebrows like María Félix came around to inspect the floors, Merced didn't blink. Did that stuck-up bitch from Mexico City, a *chilanga*, think this was Merced's first time training a new hotel worker? She'd done this many times before. The only difference was that this time she was training her daughter Alma.

Under the *chilanga's* watch, Merced showed Alma the best way to wipe down the toilet with the rags La Plaza had given her as part of her cleaning equipment. She polished the heavy imported furniture in a circular motion, slowly vacuumed the thick wool carpet, maneuvering the brush-topped hose into the dark corners and dusted the silk lampshades by hand.

"*Cuidado*," Merced warned. "*Supuestamente* this furniture is from Italy so you have to treat all these *cochinadas* like a baby."

Alma's rag slowly wiped the top of the deeply carved desk, then the porcelain base of the lamp. Her hands shook so hard she nearly pushed it off.

One by one, Merced shared all of the standard rules for La Plaza's housekeeping staff, plus a few of her own. All the while, Alma nodded and blinked with the black eyes she got from her father Donaciano. The *chilanga* watched her closely, as if Merced would give her daughter special treatment. As soon as the *chilanga* left, Merced got down to the truth—whoring.

"You think I got these nice tips just for making the beds?" Merced snorted. "You think these *desgraciados* ask for me because I'm so good at cleaning toilets?"

Alma's black eyes grew wide, but she did not blush. The full blush would come some weeks later when Merced would lay down the rules of hustling along with a glass of Presidente brandy and the room number of a waiting john.

For now, Merced kept it simple. Fold the top sheet underneath the mattress tight and smooth. No wrinkles, no creases. Those will come later when the couple who rents the room has sex. Or maybe when one of those Fort Bliss soldiers with a weekend pass comes through with one of the *cabareteras*. All along, Merced didn't mention how her eldest daughter Norma helped support the family with her job at the Tivoli cabaret in downtown Juárez. Norma spoke only of the soldiers and their whores, groping and whispering in the halls of La Plaza before slipping inside the rooms. It didn't matter now that the war was over, had been over for five years; these Bliss men had more money than ever and they spent it all here at La Plaza.

Alma blinked as her mother talked and took it all in.

After the training period ended, Alma worked on her own, and one day simply rolled into the next for Merced. Beds, beds all day long. So what if the hotel was installing these new *mugreros*, televisions or whatever these *chingaderas* were called, in the penthouse suites. So what if people like the mayor of Juárez or the Governor of Texas stayed here, *supuestamente* the finest hotel in El Paso. They were all the same.

"Pigs," Merced whispered to herself as her wet hair dripped onto her *pinche* rag of a uniform. She stripped the soft cotton sheets from the bed and a used condom fell on her rubber-soled shoe.

"*Pinche* john," she whispered. "Whore," she said as she wiped the mirror above the dressing table and finger-combed her wet hair. She barely had three minutes to wash her crotch and *culo*, but that was time enough to fog up all the mirrors in the penthouse suite.

Merced emptied the waste paper basket quickly and rushed into the marble-floored bathroom. It was bigger than her *rasquache* presidio apartment in Segundo Barrio. She inspected the room quickly. Water puddled near the clawfoot tub, and the canvas shower curtain was a little ripped at the brass rings, but that wasn't her doing. Mold and God knows what else grew in the deep scratches. Merced sucked her teeth in disgust, remembering she had put her feet down on that piece of porcelain just minutes before. She would have to scrub her body raw when she got home, then powder her toes with the athlete's foot remedy Leandro had left behind three years ago. Merced quickly wiped down the bathroom mirror, and her plump arm flapped like a little wing.

She looked at the clock. In four minutes she had to meet Alma at the service elevator. She rushed to powder the tub with Comet, swiping it down with the set of rags La Plaza Hotel had given her when she started. High-class hotel, her *nalgas*. The green-speckled powder ate away at her hands, making them itchy and stink of chlorine. After all these years as a chambermaid at the hotel, all she had to show for it were cracked, bloody hands and a heart as empty as the money jar Leandro had left in the middle of the wooden floor of their tiny apartment, vanishing down Highway 80 towards California. All the neatly rolled American bills in the mason jar had disappeared into his pocket. All the hard earnings from her paychecks at La Plaza gone, and with it her dreams for a home of her own in the Sunset neighborhood.

⚜⚜

With just a half day to make up six floors of rooms, Merced and Alma were in *joda* pushing their loaded carts down the narrow hallways and in and out of the service elevators. Sometimes, to get her mind off of her blistering feet, Merced would pretend she was one of the high-priced whores she'd seen sitting on those high-class stools, stretching out their silk-stockinged legs in the windows of the cabaret she passed by on the way to the Mercado Cuauhtémoc, their tight shiny high heels and peroxide blonde hair glowing in the sunlight. Juárez women had a name for that color—*juareña* Gold. It was a harsh, yellow-orange color, but Merced wanted it for her own hair, even if it meant being called a whore herself. Why not? She thought, smoothing out her thick black hair. These days she practically was one. Already she'd made $10 fucking one old man, a regular at the hotel who'd been waiting for her to knock. Room 303.

"There's my little spitfire," the old *sinvergüenza* said as he pulled her into the room. "My little María. *Qué bonita.*"

Merced rolled her eyes at his reference to María Félix. She'd heard it before, mainly from the *gabachos* and once from Leandro when they first met at the Mercado Cuauhtémoc. She had been selling her chiles and sweet potatoes along with the other vendors against the shaded wall of the giant *mercado,* when she first saw him in his white linen suit and matching fedora hat. He walked towards her, eyeing her like she was one of the ancho chiles laid out for his inspection.

"*Mira, la mera* María Bonita right here in Juárez," he told her, reaching for her hand.

She had seen María Félix on a movie poster at the Tivoli theater across the street from the Mercado when she had come with her husband. Her fair-skinned face set off her black hair and eyes. From then on, Merced closely read the movie star magazines, looking to see how La María wore her hair, clothes and make-up.

⚬⚬

Carefully, Merced stripped off her uniform and hung it over the chair. The *chilanga* would kill her if she saw her working in a wrinkled or ripped dress. Worse, she would probably dock her pay to have it pressed just like that one time she docked Javi after his mother forgot to iron his fancy suit covered with brass buttons and satin trim.

"Amá has to get up a half hour early just to finish ironing this *chingadera*," Javi told her once after one of the *chilanga*'s lectures. "*Pobrecita.*"

Luckily for her and Alma, they wore the same brown-gold potato sack with the plastic buttons every day. Merced looked over at her flat uniform as the old man split her legs open and entered her. Of course, fucking the old man was nothing like when she was with Leandro. For him, she took her time caressing his face, kissing him. How she loved to look into his eyes and trace the outline of his lips, stopping at the mole dancing above his upper lip. Afterwards, if there was time, she would refry some beans with the left-over bacon grease and make him some fresh flour tortillas with lard.

"Just like my grandmother's," he would say, sopping up the last of the beans with a fluffy, warm tortilla. Then Leandro would laugh and talk about Los Angeles.

"Everybody from El Paso is moving there," he'd say. "There's work in the shipyards. I'll go ahead and as soon as I find a place, I'll send for you and the girls."

Leandro neither sent word nor money. Merced had to come up with a way to support her daughters. She considered herself lucky to have met a young soldier five years ago, a Bliss man hungry for love. And then it came to her one day as she worked her rags and cursed under her breath. If she could make ten dollars in a morning off these rich *gabachos*, then her daughters should be making fifty a night.

"*No se rajen*," she told them one morning while they each ate the last of the beans and corn tortillas in the cold kitchen. "You're big girls now, *grandototas*."

"*Ay*, Mamá," Norma started, "it's too early for this."

But when Merced narrowed her eyes and stepped toward her, Norma stopped.

"You're not even pulling in half of what you're worth in the cabaret," whispered Merced as she scraped the last handful of beans out of the *olla* into Alma's bowl. "With the war over, many of those *soldados* have a lot of money saved up. You should sleep so you can look fresh for them tonight."

Norma blinked her mascara-smeared eyes. "I'm too hungry to sleep."

Before she could dip her spoon into her bowl, Merced had emptied part of her beans into Alma's bowl. "*Comételos*," Merced told Alma. "You're going to need your energy tonight."

Norma nodded. The smell of cigarettes and beer danced around her as she shook her thick gold hair, trying to wake up a little. "Today you'll need the brandy too."

"*Sí*," Merced sighed as she opened the kitchen sink cupboard and pulled out a half-filled pint bottle. "El Presidente has to go with you too."

"*¿Por qué?*" Alma asked, looking at Norma.

Norma covered her eyes with her hands. Merced cursed Leandro again under her breath and motioned for Alma to eat.

❦

With the *rebozo* tightly wrapped around her shoulders, Merced walked to the hotel with Alma. The shawl was a gift from Leandro during their first year in El Paso. She pulled it tighter around her shoulders and thought about the ones she had left back home in Chihuahua with her husband Donaciano. In the distance, the Franklin Mountains glowed in the pink dawn. It wouldn't be long before snow covered them in thick blankets. She needed a coat. And so did the girls. They needed so many things. And now, there was a way to get them.

Merced had experience with selling love. She was thankful to the first Bliss soldier she had met. After the tenth john, it wasn't so bad anymore. Today, Alma would learn. Today would be her first day earning real money, just like Merced and Norma did. As soon as they reached the Plaza Hotel's supply room, Merced and Alma began loading their carts. *La chilanga* stood by, eyeing them while mentally counting the cleaning supplies. They headed to the elevator and saw one of the bellhops, Javi, carrying heavy leather-bound suitcases. They greeted each other in passing before Merced and Alma took their carts up to the fifth floor. Merced shut her eyes and remembered what she had learned during the last five years.

First, you ask for the money right up front, or the *cabrón* could take off on you. Second, make sure he takes off all of his clothes first, just to check he isn't armed. Third, don't eat or drink anything he offers you. You never know when these men will try to poison or drug you. You had to be safe. Fourth, the moment he's done, you put your clothes on right away and shower in the next room you have to clean. That's the only time you can do this, because later on, as you clean more rooms and maybe fuck more men, you want to be a little fresh, but you don't want your skin to get all dried out with rashes.

For the past five years, Merced had repeated these rules every day like a prayer. Now, she shared this prayer with her daughter as Alma pushed her cart behind her down the carpeted hallway. Out of the corner of her eye, she watched as Alma just nodded her head and stared at her feet.

"And ask them for twenty dollars, *m'ija*," Merced said. "You're young enough, you can ask for more. How old are you telling them you are?"

"Eighteen."

"Tell them sixteen. These *descarados* want to feel like they're young studs again."

Merced could tell her daughter was biting the inside of her cheek.

"And you better not cry," Merced warned Alma, pulling out the little brown bottle of brandy. "That'll scare them away. Here."

Merced twisted the cap off the pint brandy bottle. "Take two long gulps."

On such a skinny girl, Merced knew the alcohol worked much quicker. Alma didn't spit it out like Norma did the first time she gave her some of the Presidente. Maybe Alma already had been drinking on the side, sneaking after hours into the hotel's fancy Dome Bar, like Merced did sometimes. Maybe Norma had already warned Alma. Whatever it was, Merced was glad. It made her life easier having at least one experienced daughter who liked to drink.

"*Y no te rajes,*" Merced warned her. "If I hear any screams and he's not killing you, I'll kill you myself."

Merced looked into her daughter's nodding face and saw her ex-husband Donaciano's black eyes. *Ese cabrón.* He would pay for sticking her with his *escuincles.* He was the one who wanted children, not she. But what did she know at fifteen when she married the old man? They had lived in a proper house in El Sauz, right across from the town plaza. He had wanted a family of sons to fill it, but no sons came, and wouldn't come no matter how early she rose to make tortillas, to boil the beans and to wash the clothes against the rocks of the *tajo*. God just cursed her and her old husband with two daughters. Whatever. The only time she rested was when she rode in her *comadre* Rufina's old Chevy truck the thirty miles between El Sauz and Juárez to sell Donaciano's chile pepper and sweet potato harvest. When she met Leandro, rest would come when she slept with him.

Leandro was gone now, and the Mason jar that once lay under the wooden floorboards of their brick presidio apartment was cleaned out. With the money gone, she had to fend for her daughters and herself while Leandro, that drag-ass good-for-nothing, was in Los Angeles doing who knows what, anything but sending for her and the girls.

"One day, we'll leave El Paso, too," Merced had repeated to the girls. "As soon as we get enough money to buy a house there."

Alma pulled the Presidente brandy from behind the linens in Merced's cart and took a long drink. As she leaned her head back, Merced saw herself tilting back her first brandy at the Plaza Hotel's Dome Bar on a date with Leandro. They had tucked themselves away in a far corner, distancing themselves from the snobby clientele. Her eyes watered when she remembered her burning throat and the way Leandro gently stroked her face as she coughed.

"Not so quickly," he said. "You're not a man."

"But it burns."

"*Pobrecita*," he said holding her hands. "Your hands are so cold but the brandy will warm you up."

He cupped her hands and blew on her fingers. Then he kissed her throat, tipping her head back again. Up above, she saw a glass dome made by some famous New York company. Pieces of stained glass fitted in iron whirled above her.

"Tiffany," the bartender had told them.

Against the night sky, purple and blue glass glowed with moonlight. A jungle of green leaves reached toward the center of the dome, making Merced feel like she could almost fly through the center into the stars. That night she had thought Leandro would take her to his little brick apartment in Segundo Barrio. But instead, he drove her back over the bridge, back to Chihuahua. Back to Donaciano.

"Don't get drunk," Merced told Alma. "Men want you awake and doing something."

Merced did the sign of the cross over her daughter's head before she walked into the john's room.

"Think of me," Merced told her. "And hurry. We don't have much time."

Merced watched the door close behind her daughter, then pressed her body up close, waiting until she heard Alma's muffled cries blend in with the john's murmurs.

"Okay? Okay? Okay?" the john kept asking.

What the hell, Merced thought, pounding her fist into her thigh. Just fuck her and get it over with. Didn't the john know the rules? Why was this *gabacho* so soft on her daughter? He should just break her into submission and be done with it. Merced remembered her first time with one of those traveling salesmen, a *viejo* who'd just come out of the shower. He was quick. No questions, no answers, just money.

Merced walked over to her cleaning cart, pulled out the bottle of brandy and drank until she heard the elevator announce its arrival on the fifth floor. Before Javi the bellboy and the white couple could reach her, Merced slipped the bottle back into the front pocket of the cart, where she kept the rags and industrial cleaners. Wrapping her fingers around the cold wooden handle, Merced leaned into the heavy cart and pushed. The cart rolled slowly down the hallway, passing doors with little wooden "Do Not Disturb" signs hanging on chains. Their doorknobs gleamed like giant diamonds under the hallway lights.

"*Cabrones,*" Merced whispered. "*Cabrones.*"

The couple, a man in a long wool coat and a woman in fur and silk, passed by Merced, leaving behind a trail of perfume and cologne. The man winked at her as he passed. The perfume lingered, then faded as Merced kept pushing her cart back and forth over the same stretch of carpet.

"*Ese gabacho,*" Javi said when he caught up with Merced. "The wife's a bitch. But he's a good tipper."

Merced stopped pushing her cart and stared at the bill in his hand.

"Not really."

Javi's face fell. "No?"

"You're only twenty," laughed Merced. "What do you know about tipping?"

"I know a dollar is better than fifty cents," Javi said, snapping his bill. "Lucky his wife came with him this time."

Javi started batting his eyes, putting his hand on his hips in imitation of the woman with the fur stole. "I don't want these Mexicans stealing from me, so you better tip him good," Javi screeched.

Merced and Javi's laughter could be heard down the hall, and a curious guest poked his head out of his room.

"We better leave," Javi giggled. ". . . Before they catch us."

"You're such a clown," Merced sighed as she went back to pushing her cart.

Merced took the brandy bottle from her cleaning cart once more and tilted her head back. Even before she unscrewed the cap, she felt her blood warming up, rushing like love. She'd have to get more bottles now that Alma also drank, she thought. The brandy's heat throbbed through the cotton of her dress with every step down the carpeted hallway.

When Alma finally came out of the john's room, she looked ghostly, her black eyes now a gunmetal gray.

"How much?" Merced asked, holding out her hand.

Alma put a tightly folded bill square into Merced's palm. "What is this?"

Alma reached over and unfolded the tight little square until three ten-dollar bills fanned out, almost covering her outstretched hand. Merced nodded at the money. She had never earned this much in her life. She carefully rolled the bills up and slipped them into her front pocket, where the roll hung heavy like a gun.

"Let's finish up the last room together," Merced told Alma.

The girl barely nodded and numbly followed her mother down the hall.

The brandy bottle banged against Merced's thigh, reminding her to finish it up before they left the hotel for the night. She hoped the guests in their last room had left behind a pack of cigarettes. They would go well with her drink. Once inside, she went straight to the nightstand and found a pack of Pall Malls next to two tumblers half filled with golden water and nearly melted ice. One whiff and Merced knew. Tequila. Expensive tequila. She gulped both glasses down and pulled the bottle from her apron.

"Go shower while I finish the room," she told Alma.

The tequila burned her throat. Merced reached for the pack of cigarettes and the book of matches, but before she could light up, Alma called from the bathroom with a voice that was low and desperate.

"Mamá, come here."

"*¿Qué?*" Merced.

"I can't do it," Alma sobbed.

Merced rolled her eyes. Now what? She entered the bathroom and looked down into the toilet bowl.

"Just flush it, *mensa*," Merced told Alma, who tried to squirm away from the blood.

"I can't."

Merced grabbed Alma's hand and pushed it toward the handle. Alma resisted, knocking Merced's head against the vanity. Warm liquid covered Merced's eye, dripped into her mouth and mixed with the tequila's bitterness.

⚬⚬

Shift after shift, Alma's walk slowed imperceptibly, then one day, Merced found her asleep in a closet.

"What happened?" Merced asked, shaking her daughter's shoulder.

Alma sat up but kept her eyes closed.

"I'm so tired," she said. "I just want to sleep. I don't want to walk anymore."

Anytime Alma dropped from exhaustion, she slept where she fell. After finding a Comet can with bloody fingerprints, Merced wondered if she was pregnant. One day, instead of a bottle of brandy, Merced put a Coke bottle in front of her daughter.

"Remember to use the Coca-Cola at the hotel," Merced told her before they left for the hotel that morning. "Then, when you get home, we'll give you a good washing with *perejil*."

"I don't need it," Alma said.

"Comet's not going to work," Merced told her. "Men don't want a girl who smells like a cleaning lady. Men like innocent, pure."

"Like Coke?" Alma asked looking down at her feet.

That's when Merced took the wooden spoon and smacked her across the face. If she broke her nose, she didn't care. Later, Merced would have to remember to leave Alma's face alone. Every man wanted a pretty face. The body could be bruised and bloated, but the face must be as clean and clear as a diamond. Luckily, both Norma and Alma had inherited her clear skin. No pimples, warts or scars.

Later that evening, Merced counted out the money she and Alma had earned that day. Almost $50. Already she imagined the house she would get in Boyle Heights, the neighborhood Leandro said was like Segundo Barrio but cleaner. A house with a porch and a bedroom for her and Leandro.

❧ ❧

The next morning, when they reached the hotel, the *chilanga* told them to hurry up with the rooms. "Sales convention . . . lots of men waiting."

Merced nodded grimly as she pushed her cart toward the elevator. Alma followed behind her. She would work out of Merced's cart this morning. They got out on the tenth floor and started with Room 1001.

Merced made her way to the edge of the bed, pulled out a pack of Pall Malls. She unwrapped it like a belated gift and pulled out a cigarette.

"My tip," she laughed out loud, feeling the brandy.

The match made a nice, sharp cracking sound as it ignited into a tiny flame. She took a deep breath, the smoke burning deep and long in Merced's lungs. Alma slid down the wall and sat down on the carpet with her back against the patterned wallpaper.

Before she knew it, Merced felt herself falling back on the bed, the sheets' musky smell rising and mixing with the cigarette smoke. A deep wet sob shook her body until a wail broke out of her. Choking and coughing with smoke and spit, she pushed herself up on one arm. A small string of smoke rose from the bed and spread toward the ceiling.

Alma's dark eyes spread wide like a child's. "*¡MAMÁ!!!!*"

"*Chingado,*" Merced yelled as she jumped up. She yanked the bedspread, threw it to the floor and stomped on it until the smoke stopped. The hole with its burned edges looked like a burnt-out eye socket. Merced knew the hotel wouldn't care, especially if she told the *chilanga* it was the hotel guest who had burned the hole. She also realized that she could not keep this life up. Sooner or later the hotel would figure out her little side job. Quickly, she rolled up the bedspread and tucked it under her arm like a baby.

Then she took the cigarette from her mouth and slowly began burning holes in the white cotton sheet, one-by-one until the sheet looked like it had a dozen bruised eye sockets and the room smelled of burning cotton and tobacco. The smell followed Merced into the hallway, where she kept burning holes in the bedspread under her arm. Merced didn't look down. Her eyes followed the couple walking towards her, their perfumed smell mixing with the smoke.

Before they could reach her, Merced threw the cigarette onto the floor and crushed it down into the thick carpet with her rubber-soled shoe. She kept staring at the couple, especially at the woman, who looked back at her with raised eyebrows and a red mouth frozen into an "O." Then Merced snapped open the sheet with its many eyes and laid it on the carpet in front of the couple who looked down at her and then at the sheet and then at her again.

"Mamá, wha . . ." Alma was in shock as she looked down at the sheet.

Merced followed her gaze. The burned-out eyes stared back at Merced, bruised and empty.

"*A la chingada con este hotel,*" Merced told the couple.

The man stepped out in front of the woman, her blonde head peeking over the man's shoulder every third or fourth step.

"We're leaving," Merced declared to Alma.

She grabbed the bottle of Presidente out of the cart and headed away from the service elevators. "Today."

Down in the lobby, Javi had a broad smile on his face and winked at them as they headed for the lobby's front door. Behind them, the *chilanga* was yelling something. Merced and Alma never looked back. Merced paused to lift her bottle and swig the last of the Presidente brandy, then she dropped it with a crash in front of all the *gabacho* and *mexicano* guests and workers.

Outside, the sun blared down on her, on Alma and on everybody walking toward and away from La Plaza. A car honked, and the smell of *taquitos* from the restaurant next door filled Merced's lungs. Somewhere out in Los Angeles, Leandro was waiting for her, and she had to get to him soon, or she would kill somebody. Merced looked at her daughter, still and silent under the white-hot sunshine. For a moment she saw Donaciano and then herself, still fifteen and stupid.

"Let's go get Norma," she told Alma. "We have to start packing."

"*Pero . . .*" Alma started, but Merced just kept walking away, her eyes on the horizon, the Franklin Mountains between her and the pulsing sky.

Pepper Spray

I see ya baby, Felipe thought as he sorted out his share of the mail. From behind the giant US Mail bins, he watched Angelina standing in line with some tall white guy, kissing his face, stroking his hair like he was some kind of pet dog. Angelina walked out the door to a little green Miata with white leather seats.

Sitting there like you're ready to take off into that SoCal sunset, he thought as he watched her through the slit of glass and metal that was supposed to be a window.

Who does she think she is? Just because she's going to UCLA now. Angie's as dumb as a stick but smart enough to get her new boyfriend to buy her that sweet little car that shakes its own little round ass when it takes off out of the parking lot. Probably his car, anyway.

Felipe finished sorting, lifted the mailbag strap over his shoulder. It was barely nine and already his shoulder muscles hurt as if he'd been carrying the mailbag for three hours.

Yeah, yeah, she's got those Guess jeans going on, making her Mexican ass look all heart-shaped and bouncy.

"Hey, Felipe. Quit looking out that window," Patrice yelled.

Shit. Nothing here but a bunch of ugly women. Better get his ass out to the old neighborhood. Here comes Patrice with her new wig, trying to look like Jody Watley. No way. She looks more like Bob Marley with her little fuzzy mustache. Jesus Christ. I've gotta find a better job. Soon as I get my associate's degree, I'll be lookin'.

"Hey Felipe, wanna go out to happy hour with us afterwards?" Patrice said.

"Can't," he said. "Gotta finish some work for class."

"You too old to be going to college."

"Don't even talk, old woman. You must be fifty at least."

I know you're only thirty, bitch, but don't start in on me. I get enough of this shit from Mom with her "When you gonna get married? Am I ever gonna see grandkids before I die? What was the point of having you and Carlos?"

⤛⤜

Was that catfish he smelled? Goddamn! Mom doesn't cook catfish. Must be Chondra. Is she here? Probably in Chuck's room fucking his fool head off. Mmmm! Not bad for soul food. Better than Mom's cold refried beans and stale tortillas. No beer, no tequila, just the same ol' orange Kool-Aid in that yellow Tupperware thing Mom's had since I don't know when.

"Turn off that light!" Mom yelled.

"I'm gonna watch a little TV, Mom."

"It's 12:30."

"I know."

"Don't you have to go to work tomorrow?"

Felipe popped in the latest episode of *Robotech* and lay down on the couch, imagining what the lead female character would look like. Before he could imagine how big her tits would be, he heard his brother's door open. Chondra walked into the living room in her raggedy old underwear.

"Hey, Chon."

"Hey."

She sat down on the couch across from him. What does she want? Is she gonna try something? Maybe I'll take her up on it.

"How was work?" she asked.

"Same ol' shit," Felipe said.

"Ya like the fish?"

"Pretty good."

"Angelina called."

"Yeah? What'd she say?"

"Getting married."

No way, Felipe thought. I just broke up with her six months ago. Who'd she find to marry?

"She wants you to go. Ya goin'?"

Bet she invited me to rub it in my face, Felipe thought. So what? She's only a kid. That's all she ever wanted, some guy to take care of her. And she's always trying to talk with some English accent, like she's Madonna or something. Her mom made some good *birria* though.

"I said, are you goin'?"

"You don't have to be so loud. Where's Carlos?"

"Asleep. He said you'd go."

"Why?"

"'Cause she's marrying some white guy you both knew in school, Steve something."

So she's marrying Steve. Well, fuck her, then.

⋘·⋙

"Felipe!"

"Hey Tony. Here's your bills."

"Aww, dude. How about some good mail?"

"How about this Victoria's Secret catalog?"

"Now you're talking," Tony said as he shoved the magazine into his pants.

"Just says 'resident,' but I think it's your neighbor's."

"She's a babe. Speaking of babes, I heard your ex is getting married."

How did this mofo find out about Angelina? *¡Chingado!* This neighborhood's too small.

"She's hooking up with Steve Bitchett," Felipe said.

"Bitchett? Aww, you mean Pritchett. The guy who used to wear high waters?"

"Who would've thought she liked that geekazoid."

"She liked you," Tony said.

Low blow. Yeah, I'm into *Robotech* and *Star Wars*. And yeah, I go dressed up like a Jedi Knight to LA Con. And, sure, I stay up all night watching the "Star Wars" movies but at least I'm not one of those Trekkie weirdos. And I'm not into Rubik's Cube or chess like this Steve guy. Let her marry the *gabacho*.

"If you go, I'll see you there," Tony said.

"You goin'?"

Felipe's bag almost fell off his shoulder.

"Adela's known her since high school. So, you know, I gotta go," Tony said.

Felipe nodded and started walking toward his mail truck. "Are the other guys going?"

"Only Mario," Tony said, adjusting the magazine. "He's the best man."

So even the best quarterback that ever played for Garfield High was going.

After leaving Tony's house, Felipe drove to the next stop on his route, Han's Liquor Store. "Han Solo" Felipe used to call him until Han got his mail-order bride from Korea. She looked just like a doll. One time Felipe made a play for her, but she pushed him away. And then Han attacked him with a broomstick. Felipe backed out of the tiny store and swore to himself he'd never bother her again. That cute little China doll never came out of her dollhouse in Monterey Park and never worked in Han's store again. For a while, Felipe thought she'd gone back to Korea or died. It turned out she had a baby.

Another time, while he was doing his route, Felipe saw her pushing a baby carriage. He almost caught up with her, but she saw him and took off across Atlantic Boulevard. She didn't even wait for the light to turn green.

Han eventually got over Felipe's loutish flirtation during the riots that broke out after the cops had assaulted Rodney King. They mainly took place in South Central but a bunch of teenagers tried to start something up in front of Han's store.

"Go away!" Han yelled at them, holding up that stupid broomstick. "Call police!"

Felipe could see the sweat shining on Han's forehead and the broomstick shaking in his hands. As the kids started walking up to him, one guy, El Sleepy, started doing a duck walk and stretching his eyes with his fingers.

"Ching, chong, chink," he sang as he walked like a penguin. "Ching, chong, chink."

When Han was about to swing the stick, Felipe walked up in front of the boys.

"Get the fuck outta here, mailman," El Sleepy said.

Felipe pulled out his regulation pepper spray, and Cobra and Jelly Beans stepped back.

"*Órale, chamacos,*" he said, "step off, or you'll be crying like babies in a couple of seconds."

When Felipe saw Cobra reach into his pants, he let them have it. Jelly Beans took off, but Cobra and El Sleepy just screamed and cried. Then Han started beating them with his broomstick. He kept swatting the two boys, even while Felipe tried grabbing his arms. Before the cops came, Felipe pulled the stick out of Han's hands. Instead of hauling those punks away, the cops called the paramedics to clean them up. Felipe couldn't believe it. Then, one of the cops started grilling him about why he used the pepper spray.

"Self-defense, man," Felipe said.

"How about the *chino* beating those kids up with the stick?"

"They're lying."

The cops finally took Cobra and El Sleepy away. Han went inside the store and turned off the lights. When Felipe heard his car coming out of the driveway, he thought for sure Han would stop to shake his hand. But Han just took off and drove back to his pretty China doll in Monterey Park.

After that incident, every time Felipe dropped off Han's mail, Han gave him free Cokes and let him sit under the air conditioning in the hot summers.

One day, after Felipe handed Han his mail, Han showed him the rifle he kept under the counter.

"No more broom?" Felipe asked.

"Fuck broom. Nobody mess with me now."

"Just don't shoot me, okay?" Felipe picked up his bag and started walking back to his truck.

"Felipe!" Han yelled.

"What?"

"Have a drink sometime."

"Yeah, yeah, sometime."

"Maybe tomorrow?"

"I have a wedding tomorrow."

Then he said something in Korean.

"What?"

"Congratulations," Han said.

✦✦

Sitting in one of the booths in the back of the Silver Dollar bar, Felipe snuggled up to Mauve, trying to see if he could get worked up over her, the way he used to with other girls. He hadn't been laid in seven months and jacking off didn't cut it anymore. So, did he want to take this girl to Angelina's wedding? Mauve had nothing on Angelina. Bad skin. Fat ass. She had nice hair, though.

After a couple of beers, Mauve was getting friendly. But when she put her hand on his knee, Felipe jumped up and went to the bathroom. He splashed cold water on his face.

"Goddamn, she's ugly," he whispered.

There wasn't enough beer in the world to make this girl sexy. Felipe thought of Han's wife, with her small feet and clear, glowing skin. Maybe it was time for him to get a mail-order bride for himself. He remembered someone had paid $5,000 for a Russian girl who looked like a model. It was a really old guy too, with no hair and green slimy teeth. Felipe looked at his hair. Not bad. It was graying out but at least he wasn't bald. And his skin. Blaagh. What did Mom call him? Orange face? Just then, he noticed a tomato stain on his white shirt. He'd love to have Mom wash it, but she'd let him have it about being a slob and how no woman was ever gonna want him.

"Go to the pueblo," she kept saying, referring to her small village in Zacatecas. "You'll find someone decent who'll love you for taking care of her."

Felipe didn't want to end up like Don Emilio, that old guy on his route who lived alone in a stinky house and no grandkids. Did he really want to pay for a wife? He continued to look in the men's room mirror. Maybe one of those video dating services or the personals would help.

"Maybe you'll meet somebody nice at Angelina's wedding," he remembered his mom suggesting.

"I already met somebody nice."

"You mean pizza face?"

Like his mother was Michelle Pfeiffer or something.

"How did you meet Dad?" Felipe remembered asking her.

"Through your *tía* Ofelia. She introduced him to me at your cousin's baptism."

"I don't go to baptisms."

"Maybe you should."

When he got back to the booth, there were two Jack and Cokes sitting in front of Mauve.

"Thought you might want another round." She smiled, then giggled.

Felipe sat down at the edge of his seat. From the corner of his eye, he looked at her boobs practically falling out of the low-cut tank top.

"I'm a little tired today," he said.

"All that walking, huh?"

"You know how it is for us mailmen."

He took a sip of his drink and got up. Mauve slowly drank hers until Felipe sat down again, his leg on the outer edge of the booth. Mauve slid over to him, grabbed his face with both hands and tried to kiss him. Felipe stood up and wiped his mouth.

"C'mon. I'll take you home."

⤳ ⤳

Two fuckin' hours. Who has a wedding for two fucking hours? Felipe should've known. Before they broke up, Angelina was always talking about her "dream" wedding, like she was Barbie or something, telling him how she wanted to "do it right:" big Catholic church, ten bridesmaids, ten groomsmen, priest, altar boys—the works! She got the ideas from those magazines. When she first showed him *Bride*, he couldn't believe his eyes: picture after picture of some chick looking drugged out in her big white dress.

"No way," Felipe told her. "No way am I paying for all that."

"But my parents can't afford this." She pointed to a dress by someone named Vera Wang.

"Tough shit," he said. "I'm a mailman, not Donald Trump."

"But you can take a loan out," she said with a straight face.

"You take a loan out."

It was pretty much over after that. Angelina was not going to date this poor Mexican slob of a mailman. So now, she was hooking up with Steve, one of five white guys in his high school who was a total geek. Felipe guessed Steve had some kind of a real job after graduating from UCLA.

When the priest asked if anyone had any reason why these two dopes shouldn't be "joined," nobody said a damn thing. Nobody thought there was a problem. Felipe did. Hell yeah, he did. But what was he going to do about it? This wasn't *Four Weddings and a Funeral*, and he wasn't Hugh Grant, that's for sure. Felipe gripped his little can of regulation pepper spray in the pocket of his gray slacks. It felt warm and friendly. How many times had it saved his ass?

When Steve raised the veil from Angelina's face, Felipe took a deep breath. She still looked seventeen, all fresh and pretty. He couldn't stand to look at Mauve, who was leaning in so close to him, he could smell her sweat brewing with her perfume.

"I love her dress," Mauve whispered.

Before the priest ended the ceremony, he pointed to the blank wall above the giant portrait of the Virgen de Guadalupe.

"The bride and groom would like to share with you through pictures the reasons they fell in love."

Journey's "Faithfully" whined through the speakers while, on the wall, slides of Steve and Angelina as kids popped up. When they flashed a picture of Angelina in her prom dress, Felipe's heart busted. He had asked her to that prom, but she'd turned him down. So he went "stag" with Tony and Mario and watched her dance with some kid from another high school. "Rhythm of the Night" was the theme, and the DJ kept playing that song by DeBarge every five minutes. For years after the prom, whenever he heard that song, he flipped the radio station.

The next slide nearly killed Felipe. It was the picture of Angelina at Huntington Beach. You could tell part of it had been cut off, and he knew why. It used to be him sitting there next to her, throwing his head back laughing. She was smiling up at the camera. By the time the next picture came up, Felipe was crying.

"I always cry at weddings too," Mauve said, leaning her head on his shoulder, wrapping her arm around his.

Was it the slides or Mauve with her pizza-skin face leaning on him? Or maybe it was Han's China doll and her baby? Whatever it was, it was enough to make Felipe break out his pepper spray for the second time in a month and spray the bride and groom as they walked down the aisle. Then it was like Han with his broom. Felipe just kept spraying, even while the best man and a groomsman tried to push him down into the red carpet. Some of the spray got into his eyes. But he kept pressing on the button until he heard the little "ssst" of the empty can.

Around him, women screamed, men yelled, little kids ran up and down the aisle. Soon, the cops were there. This time, instead of dragging off punks like Cobra and El Sleepy, they cuffed and dragged him screaming out of the church. The cops threw Felipe down on the sidewalk, where they waited for the paramedics to wash his eyes out.

"Why'd you do this? Who are you? Where'd you get the pepper spray?" they yelled at him.

Felipe twisted around like a slug sprinkled with salt while the sidewalk burned through his clothes. He heard Angelina whimpering and Steve cursing. For a second, he thought he heard Mauve laughing. Sirens down the street got louder and louder. And for the first time since that day at the beach with Angelina, Felipe smiled into the sun beating on his face.

Matadora

The scorched Aztec remains of La Quemada rose up as Luis and Teresa drove over the lonely road to Zacatecas. Rocky hills and sparse grass glowed orange in the setting sun.

If only she would be quiet and let me think. Jesus, just let me think. What am I gonna do? What am I gonna do? Look at the Quemada? Ugh. I can't. Have to get to Zacatecas and this road is as windy as fuck. Everything's dry, dry, dry. It's like fire all around me.

The road wound and curved like loose coils. While Teresa discussed the history of the stone ruins, she twisted the gold wedding band around her finger. Luis could almost hear the metal sliding over the skin of her thin finger. Then she grew quiet.

God, please don't cry, Luis thought. He knew if he turned to her, she would start bawling. I can't take it anymore, he screamed in his head. But all Teresa heard was silence. Luis pressed down hard on the pedal, then bit his lip. As the road widened, turn-of-the-century houses and apartment buildings began to emerge, eventually giving away to brick and white-washed colonial buildings.

"What time is it?" Luis asked.

Instead of answering, Teresa looked out the window.

Shit, now what? Does she know about my appointment with Romelia? Did she see that when she scrolled through my text messages and Facebook? How the heck did she find the credit card charge for the three sets of teddy lingerie I bought Romelia?

Fives! We met at five in the afternoon. We kissed at five in the morning. We fucked in five hotel rooms. And, now, the fifth is coming up during my brother's wedding.

In the distance, Zacateca's main cathedral, dedicated to La Virgen de la Asunción, loomed up, its pink stone shining in the rays of the orange sun. Angels, virgins, saints cascaded down the front of its elaborately carved façade.

"That's supposed to look like a tabernacle," Teresa said, tapping her finger against the window.

Luis looked up, blinking. "Huh? What tabernacle?"

"It's supposed to be that little gold box behind the altar where the priest keeps the wine and wafers."

"Oh." Luis looked back at the winding road.

"Maybe we can visit it before we have to get to your brother's wedding?"

Luis said nothing.

When they arrived at the Hotel Quinta Real, Teresa waited eagerly for Luis to admire the hotel's appearance. The hotel had been built around the city's former main bullring, a stone structure rising five stories high. It was one of the reasons she reserved a room there. Carefully placed lights lit up the gold-tinted stones and the delicately arched windows. A colonial-style brick building built into the ring served as the hotel's main entrance.

"Welcome to Hotel Quinta Real," said the woman at the check-in counter.

"No wonder it costs so much," Luis said, looking at the El Cubo aqueduct running across the front of the hotel.

Once in their room, Luis dropped their suitcases and immediately headed back to the lobby, to buy some cigarettes, he said. As soon as he got to the lobby, he pulled out his phone. The concierge waved at him. Luis quickly turned his back to him and called Romelia's cell phone.

"You made it," she laughed. "Five on the dot."

As they spoke, he twisted his wedding band with the fingers of his free hand.

"When are you coming in?" Luis asked.

The concierge walked towards him, waving.

"We can call you a cab," the concierge said so loudly he drowned out Romelia.

Luis shook his head and walked toward the bullring. Hundreds of round tables glowed with candlelight in what was once the ring. Battery-operated lights installed underneath the tables blazed through the white tablecloths. As soon as he saw the waiters rolling out the white tiered cake, he knew.

⁂

After Luis left their hotel room, Teresa pulled out a bottle of Siete Leguas tequila from her suitcase. The vendor in Guadalajara had assured her that this brand was sold as El Patrón, her favorite, in the United States. She poured a quarter inch into her water glass and took a sip, savoring the burn in her throat.

Teresa went to her bag and took out the dress she would be wearing as maid of honor the day after next. The long blue velvet dress needed to be pressed. It was a floor-length gown with a scooped collar, tight-fitting basque and long sleeves. When Hilary Clinton was still the first lady, she wore a similar dress when she was featured on the cover of *Vanity Fair*.

Hilary had seemed especially dignified in that picture, wearing a simple pearl necklace and pearl drop earrings.

Teresa laid out the pearl necklace, a gift from Luis, against the navy dress. Luis had given her the necklace during their honeymoon in Santa Barbara. She hoped to find some gold earrings while in Zacatecas but doubted she could in this town known for its silver barons and mines.

After pouring out more tequila, Teresa walked out onto the balcony and looked at the city lights glimmering like diamonds on black velvet. She shuddered before gulping down the clear liquid. She still could not get the image of Luis talking to Romelia out of her head. She noticed the soft look in his eyes and the tender curve of his mouth as he spoke to that woman, an old college friend. Teresa had caught him once before talking to that "friend" late at night when she woke up to find him gone from her side. In the living room, she had heard him whispering, saying, "I can't wait to kiss you again." Her heart froze at that moment. Then he pulled down his sweatpants, took out his penis and started masturbating. Teresa's heart pounded in her ears.

"What are you doing?" she screamed.

Luis jumped up and fumbled, pulling up his pants.

"I'll call you later," he whispered.

"What are you doing?"

Luis silently placed the phone back into the receiver. Suddenly, Teresa burst out crying.

"But I wasn't hard yet," Luis mumbled as he walked back to their bedroom.

Teresa followed him, sobbing into her hands.

The next day, Luis left for his office without speaking to her, not even after she kissed the top of his head. For the rest of the day, she tried to focus on her students and their presentations on Chicano authors, but all she could see was her husband's penis. She laughed a little at the memory of his words but then silenced herself. This isn't funny, she thought. This isn't anything.

The memory slowly faded as Teresa poured another quarter inch of tequila and went to bed alone. Outside beyond the balcony, she could hear the night pulsating with footsteps and laughter. She thought she heard Luis' voice in the distance and the faint sound of a woman giggling.

⋙·⋘

When the wedding announcement came, Teresa was ready. She braced herself for Luis' contempt.

Instead, he held his brother's invitation with the raised script in both hands and said, "We're going."

"Oh, great. . . ."

"And there's a note here from Manuel. . . . He says his Karina wants you to be the maid of honor . . . and wear blue velvet."

"Oh, I love the idea of velvet, especially for a December wedding. Rich and warm, it will blend with the wintry weather," Teresa exclaimed in delight.

⋙·⋘

The next day, while Luis showered, Teresa slipped into the cobblestone alley that ran past the hotel. White-washed buildings built during the Spanish colonial period rose up around her. A wooden sign with the word "Joyería" swayed in the cold wind. The jewelry store's warm air wrapped her up like a quilt when she walked inside. She immediately turned to the glass counter filled with glittering jewels, where a pair of garnet earrings twinkled.

Teresa breathed deeply. Pearl bracelets, delicate silver chains in a fishbone pattern and silver rings gripping a rainbow of semi-precious stones glittered under the glass of the counter, but the blood-colored stones stood out. Suddenly, a cloud of Coco Chanel perfume overtook Teresa.

"*Buenos días,*" said a blonde woman behind the glass counter.

The woman immediately reminded her of Tía Lola, who loved to wear perfume and dyed her hair until it was platinum blonde. Tía was shameless, but Uncle Pepe adored her.

Tía Lola wore pearl earrings, Teresa remembered. For a moment, she considered the creamy jewel. But the garnet glimmered and beckoned to her.

The attendant presented herself as Coco and asked, "*¿Qué se le ofrece?*"

"I'd like to see those earrings."

"*¿Cuáles? ¿Estos?*" the woman asked, picking up some emerald teardrop earrings.

"*Esos, los de* 'garnet,'" Teresa said, half-ashamed she didn't know the Spanish word for the stone.

"Ah, the blood-red ones. In my opinion, these are more precious than rubies," Coco volunteered.

Teresa smiled uncontrollably as she held up the red stones to the light. Although both were heart-shaped, they were not identical. One was a little larger and a little more lopsided. Both were set in filigree silver. Yes, much better than rubies, she thought as she poked the posts through her earlobes.

"*Qué bonitos,*" Coco said as she brought over a hand mirror.

Teresa giggled.

"Like blood mixed with sun rays," Teresa said, smiling.

Coco laughed. "It depends whose blood it is."

Teresa laughed and thought she wouldn't mind seeing Luis' blood on the earrings.

"Where are you staying?" Coco asked.

"La Quinta Real."

"Ah," Coco mouthed with her red lips. "*La plaza de toros.*"

Teresa nodded, the heat and perfume drugging her by the second.

"That's where blood rules," Coco continued.

Right then and there, she knew she should buy them, no matter how much Luis would complain. She tightened the screws a little more.

"*¿Cuánto?*" Teresa said, pulling out her wallet.

Coco eyed her from beneath her mascaraed lashes. "*Cincuenta.*"

Teresa thought Coco was giving her a deal at fifty pesos.

"*Dólares,*" Coco laughed.

Teresa grimaced as she pulled out a fifty-dollar bill from her purse, knowing Luis would moan about the cost.

Before she knew it, Coco leaned in and kissed her on the cheek. Teresa saw the red lip marks reflected on the glass counter. Then, Coco's soft perfumed hand caressed her cheek. This time the Chanel scent exploded into her nostrils.

"*Vaya, m'ija,*" Coco said. "Sometimes you have to kiss the bull before you kill it."

Once she left the jewelry store, Teresa felt the streets of Zacatecas closing in on her. Feeling faint, she leaned hard against the doors of the cathedral and pushed one open. Inside, her dizziness and the darkness blinded her. The scent of copal invaded her nostrils as a darkness fell over her. She sank down onto the marble floor.

☙ ❧

Like the night before, the white linen tables lit up the former bullring around a wooden dance floor, where guests danced to "Bidi Bidi Bom Bom" by Selena. Luis was dancing with Romelia. His brother Manuel and his bride Karina danced alongside them. Luis hadn't danced since his own wedding and had forgotten how good it was to dance with a woman who was not always falling down drunk. Romelia moved close to him, her breath sweet with buttery frosting from the wedding cake. Her eyes looked straight into his. They were not glazed with tequila, her movements were crisp, unaffected by overindulgence.

Bailen, bailen, cabrones, Teresa thought as she observed them and sipped the last of her tequila shot. She felt the warmth of the liquor throughout her body, now heating her earlobes set afire by the garnet earrings.

"Time to kiss the bull," she said to herself as she walked up to the band.

When Luis heard the first few notes of "*Sabor a mí,*" he knew Teresa was drunker than he expected. He also knew that his family expected him to dance with his wife, no matter how drunk she was.

Teresa walked up to the couple on the dance floor, her blue velvet dress shimmering in the light from an overhead disco ball festooned with tiny mirrors.

"Sometimes the wife doesn't want to dance with her husband," Teresa jeered at Luis and turned to Romelia. "Sometimes she wants to dance with the girlfriend."

"*Tanto tiempo disfrutando de este amor,*" sang a female crooner on the band stand.

Romelia smiled and stared into Teresa's eyes. Luis froze.

"You don't have to do this," Luis said. "Please don't."

"It's all right, Luis," Romelia smiled. "I've danced with women before."

134

Yes, but not in front of my family, Luis thought.

Teresa grabbed Romelia's left hand and assumed the male dance position. She swayed her from side to side, smiling and laughing.

"*No pretendo, ser tu dueño,*" the singer crooned the familiar lyrics.

Teresa had reacted to the lyrics, agreeing that she had outright possessed Luis; she owned him. She smiled with the knowledge that Romelia could never own him. Romelia accepted this. Suddenly, the empty tables seemed to spin in place. All the guests, including her mother-in-law, were up and dancing to the bolero. Teresa skillfully led Romelia around the floor. Maybe she wasn't that drunk. At one point, she dipped Luis' mistress so deeply, her breasts bulged out from her décolleté evening gown. Teresa's garnets burned through her black hair.

Sweat dripped down from Luis' forehead. Everybody around him was laughing and clapping. They thought it was a joke, but Luis knew it was a game. His brother and his new bride not only watched but danced along with his wife and his mistress. The song, mixing with the laughter and the chatter, bounced off the walls, numbing Luis with each note. When the song ended, Teresa pulled back and looked at Romelia. Luis closed his eyes, but when he opened them again, Teresa was hugging Romelia. Hard. And before he could stop her, Teresa kissed Romelia long and hard on the lips. Romelia pulled back, but Teresa held her head still. Most of the guests gasped, but some young men clapped. The band played on.

Luis strode up to the couple and pulled Romelia away. Teresa watched them recede, her chest rising and falling. She breathed deeply, but her lungs felt shallow. Slowly, she pushed her way through the dancing couples, making it back to their table. Luis and Romelia were gone, but his mother remained, her shot glass refilled.

Teresa picked up the glass and sipped the tequila.

"You kissed the bull," her mother-in-law, Marta, laughed.

"I kissed the bull," Teresa whispered, then let her face fall into her hands.

Outside of the hotel, Luis could feel a pricking in the back of his neck. Sharp pain shot down his back and brought him down.

"*Amor*," Romelia said and dragged him into the hotel lobby. "*¡Ayúdame!*" she cried to the concierge standing near the doorway.

He quickly walked over to her and helped seat Luis on a lobby sofa.

"What's wrong?" Romelia asked him.

Luis was choking, could not speak. His tongue felt numb, as if it had been cut off. Around him people watched as the concierge opened the collar of his tuxedo shirt and pulled his tie off. A blonde woman with garnet earrings pushed her way into the circle of people. When she leaned over him, the scent of Coco Chanel revived him.

Luis thought he heard her say, "*Vaya*."

No Such Thing

The moment the theater lights dimmed and he shoved a clump of warm buttery popcorn into his mouth, it was like the start of a vacation for Jesús. Anything was possible.

Tonight's possibility was *Bad Education*, Almodóvar's latest, this time with an up-close and personal look at the Catholic Church. Screeching, *Psycho*-like violins played during the opening credits over black and white photos of drag queens with thick mascara and full lips, crosses and little boys.

An old white couple walked in front of him, one row over. The old man shuffled while his wife, walking a little faster, pushed his elbow. Jesús' vacation was being interrupted. As soon as the couple sat down, Jesús got up and moved down a row to see the entire screen without obstruction. The Mexican actor portraying the lead drag queen made every hair on his body vibrate. How could Gael García Bernal go from a scruffy, horny, pothead teen in one movie to a hairy Che Guevara in another and to this wonderful creature now?

"Beautiful," Jesús whispered before biting into another popcorn kernel.

When the actor lay on his lover's bed as he took it from behind, Jesús felt the sweat trickle from his armpits.

Thank God for Almodóvar. Someday, Jesús would go to Spain and thank the man for showing real gay men on the screen. Men who loved other men and weren't afraid to die for that love. Besides, there was nothing like a macho Mexican getting it up the ass and loving it.

"*Viejo sinvergüenza*," Jesús could hear his mother sputter.

He looked harder into Gael's eyes. Yes, he looked a little like Mamá, especially with that blonde wig. For a while, he could only think about her, telling him to get his taxes done.

Jesús closed his eyes for a bit and thought of Don, who was working in the bookstore this afternoon and tonight would join him for a nice quiet dinner, maybe a couple of beers and then a movie, maybe *Supersize Me* or *Election*. Just no talk about the bookstore. Anything but that.

After the movie, Jesús drove over to Safeway for a couple of six-packs before heading back to his Monterey Park apartment.

"This is why you're getting that *panza*," Mamá said during one Sunday visit. "Too much *cerveza*. You're going to end up just like your father."

"Don't listen to this crazy *vieja*, *m'ijo*," his father said as he grabbed his mother around her waist. "She loves my *panza*."

"*Payaso*," Mamá said, pushing her husband away. "Jesús'll never find a nice-looking wife looking like a fatso."

Jesús ran to the kitchen as soon as he got to his apartment. He opened a can of Olympia and poured it into one of the pilsner glasses he kept in the freezer. Jesús drank half the glass in one gulp.

After taking a deep breath, Jesús closed his eyes and drank the rest.

While working on a second can, he pulled out two DVDs from his collection. Before he could pop in *Women on the Verge of a Nervous Breakdown*, he noticed his laptop was open. He wiped his fingers on his shorts but some beer smeared on the touchpad.

"Well, fuck."

A new email from Don read, "Come quick!"

Before he left, Jesús took a beer can from the freezer, then grabbed another. Might as well feel good before Don lowers the boom.

Don was locking up by the time Jesús got to the store. Under the fluorescent lights Don looked almost albino. Jesús stopped just before he reached the door. As Don pushed the cart weighted with books, his long skinny body and bald head were bent like that old man's at the movies.

"I can smell the beer," Don said as he relocked the door behind Jesús.

"I only had one."

"How was the movie?"

"Spiritual," Jesús said, remembering Gael's eyes. "But at the same time disturbing."

"So, the usual Almodóvar experience."

Don opened the door to the back office. The spreadsheet winked onto the computer screen as soon as he touched the mouse.

"We're not gonna make it this year, are we?" Jesús asked. The gas bloating his stomach was pumping into his head.

He looked at the numbers Don highlighted in red and remembered Mamá telling him that he should work with his brother at the Ford plant in Long Beach. That way, Jesús could finally settle down with a nice wife, have a family and stop fooling around with this nonsense about owning his own business.

"And a bookstore, too!" Mamá said. "Who reads in East LA?"

She asked him why Don was involved.

"He has a master's degree and the money," Jesús said.

"A master's degree, huh?" Mamá said. "And money too? That's good. But don't come to me if you guys go broke, because I don't have any money left after paying for your college. And with your father on disability, ooof!"

That was Mamá's favorite expression: "Ooof!"

"We need a loan," Jesús said as he scrolled through the spreadsheet.

"I'm tapped out, and you know the bank isn't going to shell out any more money," Don said.

"Maybe my mother will. I can probably get her to lend us a couple of thousand."

Don put his hands up in the air and sighed. "Why do you want to do that?"

"She owes me."

"When are you gonna get over that?"

"When she dies."

⇜ ⇝

At sixteen Jesús knew he was onto something when he first saw Almodóvar's *Law of Desire* at Laemmle's Cinemas in downtown LA.

"Take your clothes off," an off-camera voice asked a young and tender Spanish actor. "Go to the mirror and kiss yourself."

The actor did this, smiling a little as the voice asked him to touch his asshole. When the voice told him to get ready for anal sex, Jesús shoved a handful of popcorn into his mouth and twisted his legs tight. Popcorn never tasted saltier.

"Don't look at me!" the voice said as soon as the actor turned his head back toward the camera.

But it was the final scene that did it for Jesús, when a youthful Antonio Banderas died in the arms of his lover, looking like Christ in the Virgin Mary's arms as sculpted by Michelangelo.

Jesús' head felt like a balloon as he floated toward the exit. Outside, he boarded the number 18 bus and took it all the way back to Whittier Boulevard, back to the barrio. As the bus drove through Skid Row, he saw the hustlers dressed in their short shorts and halter tops standing on the sidewalks. He could almost smell the piss on the alley walls. A Chicano hustler in a blonde wig and white tube top got on the bus. Whistles and "*Oye, joto*" flew from some of the passengers but stopped when Blondie sat down next to Jesús.

"*Qué calor, ¿no?*" Blondie said. His fingernails flashed red as he fanned himself.

Chanel's Coco—his mother's favorite perfume—filled the bus. Jesús turned to the hustler, who quickly smiled at him. Stubble poked through the thick make-up and his eyebrows had been thinned down to little lines that curved like upside down Cs. Just like his mother's.

Jesús kept his body turned toward the window until the bus stopped at First Street. He felt Blondie get up and heard him walk to the front of the bus. It was safe now, he thought, as he slowly turned to watch Blondie bob up and down, his ass bouncing on thin brown legs down the aisle. Just before getting off, Blondie blew him a kiss.

Jesús snorted.

He watched Blondie walk into La Rondalla, a bar frequented by Mexican men in cowboy hats and huge belt buckles.

As soon as he got home, Jesús changed into his pajamas and stumbled into the bathroom. As he flossed his teeth, he got closer and closer to the mirror over the sink. He closed his eyes and imagined Antonio Banderas in front of him.

"Antonio," he said, then kissed the mirror. For a moment, Jesús thought he saw someone walk by. Then, the floss cut into his gums as his arm jerked back.

"Who's Antonio? What are you saying?" Mamá said, her thin eyebrows arched so high, she looked frightened.

"Nobody, Mamá," Jesús said, "just an actor in a movie."

"I'll show you an actor. Get to bed."

He heard her mutter something about his father cutting off his balls if he ever found out.

❦ ❦

On the last day of their Going-Out-Of-Business sale, Don took Jesús' mother by the hand and started showing her around the bookstore. Before Jesús could stop him, Don took her straight to the Gay and Lesbian section.

"What's this?" Mamá said.

"It's the gay section," Don said.

"What? A section for *maricones*?"

Jesús motioned for Don to go back to the cash register. Don stood still for a moment before shaking his head and walking away.

"Writers like Gil Cuadros, Gloria Anzaldúa, Luis Alfaro," Jesús said. "They're famous in Chicano literature."

"Mexican *maricones*? There's no such thing."

"Don't use that word, Mamá. It's rude."

Mamá walked over to the biographies and stood right in front of the Elvis section. "They know he's dead, don't they?" Mamá said. She looked over at the woman who was holding an Elvis book.

"Don't give me that, Mamá," Jesús said. "You know you still play his records."

"What a waste," she said and pulled out a book on Marilyn Monroe.

"Dead," Mamá said and threw the book on the floor.

John F. Kennedy.

"Dead."

Jackie O.

"Dead."

María Félix.

"Dead, but not forgotten."

It was the only one Mamá held onto as she kept pulling out books while Jesús kept re-shelving them.

"Why did you even bother coming, Mamá?" Jesús said. "Why?"

"See, this is your problem. Too many books on dead people." Then she walked over to the fiction section.

"What's this?" Mamá said. "Is your bookstore too good for Mexican writers who aren't *maricones*?"

Jesús pointed to the Chicano literature sign.

"Aren't they good enough to mix with your gringos?" Mamá asked.

Jesús walked over to Don, who was finishing up with the Elvis fan at the register.

"How are we doing?" Jesús asked.

"Not so good. We're barely going to cover stock."

Jesús looked around the store. Every shelf looked full, except for the Mystery/Horror section, which had sold out of everything, including the used books. Not even a month of selling this stuff at half off would pull them out of the hole they were in. Jesús reached over and squeezed Don's hand.

"How's your mother doing?" Don asked.

"I think she's taking it harder than we are."

Mamá walked over to a rocking chair in the children's section and started reading her María Félix biography.

"Have you told her we're moving in together?" Don said. His forehead sparkled with sweat.

"I'll tell her after the sale. I promise."

Don slammed the cash drawer shut. Jesús looked over at Mamá.

"I give up," Don said and walked to the back office.

Two students walked in just as Jesús was about to go after him.

"Hey," Goth girl said, "do you have an anime section?"

"Yeah, it's over there, under the 'Anime' sign."

"Do you have *Lonely Shogun Monk*?" asked the boy with an Abercrombie shirt.

Jesús walked over to the anime shelf to pull out the book but saw the gun before he made it back to the register.

"Open it up," Abercrombie boy said while Goth girl locked the door.

Jesús felt his head fill with sand when he heard the door lock click shut. The gun looked like a dead crow in the boy's hand, the beak opened wide and round.

"That's not gonna work," Jesús said. But he sounded like he was talking and breathing through a feather pillow.

"Shut up," the boy said and cocked the gun.

Mamá kept rocking and reading.

"Hurry up," Goth girl said.

Jesús thought he could smell Chanel through the pillow feathers filling his nose and mouth but kept putting the cash from the compartments of the register into Abercrombie boy's hand. From the corner of his eye he thought he saw Goth girl move down the aisle of shelves.

"Why are you so quiet?" Mamá said as she came up to Jesús.

"Mamá."

Goth girl came up to her and smiled. "This your mamá?" she said. "She know a robbery when she sees one?"

"I know one," Mamá said. She clutched the María Félix book to her chest. "I know a lot of things."

Abercrombie boy stashed the cash in his backpack and pointed the crow at Jesús' face. "Okay, now turn around and get behind the counter."

Jesús stumbled behind the counter, holding on to the book cart.

"What?" Mamá said. "Me too?"

"You too, you old bitch."

Mamá looked at Jesús and tilted her head.

"Do what he says, Mamá," his voice said in deep, slow motion.

From there, they watched as the girl shoved graphic novels into the backpack. Before the thieves left, the girl blew Jesús a kiss that completely suffocated him. He fainted. When he came to, Don and Mamá were kneeling over him.

"How could you let that boy talk to me like that?" Mamá said. "And that girl . . ."

"Are you okay? What happened?" Don said, looking at the empty register drawer.

"We were robbed," Jesús said, his voice back to normal.

"What? Why didn't you call me?" Don said as he held Jesús's head and stroked his face.

"Don't let me go," Jesús said.

Don leaned his face close to Jesús'.

Jesús heard Mamá as she ran into the back office and called the police.

"I guess Mamá knows now," Don said.

Mamá didn't come out until she heard the officer come into the store.

༺ ༻

On the night before they were supposed to turn in their keys to the landlord, Mamá helped them pack the leftover books, zipping so much packing tape over cardboard boxes, Jesús knew he'd need a box cutter to open them. She wouldn't look at Don, who took each box, wrote the author names and stacked them on the dolly.

"Hope you guys sold enough of this shit to pay your rent," Mamá said.

"You don't have to do this, Amelia," Don said. "We can pack it all ourselves."

"No, no," she said. "I need to help my son and his . . . friends."

"I'll go get the truck," Jesús said.

Mamá looked up at him but quickly went back to taping the last of the boxes.

Inside the truck, Jesús popped in his *Bad Education* CD while Sarita Montiel sang "*Quizás, quizás, quizás.*" The back of the truck shook a little as Don shoved the last of the boxes into the bed. Don opened the passenger door.

"Ready?" he asked.

"I'm never going to be ready."

Don looked back at the door to the back of their bookstore. Then, he leaned over and kissed Jesús on the lips. When Don leaned back, Jesús could see his mother standing at the open doorway.

"Just lock the door and go home, Mamá," Jesús said. "We'll be back soon."

After unloading the boxes at the storage center, Jesús and Don took the long way back to the bookstore.

"After all this," Jesús said, "we need a vacation."

"We can't afford a vacation."

"Yeah, we can."

"How? Where?"

"Spain."

"You've been watching too much Almodóvar."

"Why not? We can use the insurance money."

Jesús parked in front of the bookstore.

"I'll see you back at your place," Don said.

Jesús watched him walk back to his Impala. It was white and shiny, just like Don. Sarita Montiel sang her high-pitched version of "*Maniquí Parisien.*" Jesús listened with his eyes closed before getting out.

Seeing the For Lease sign in the front of his bookstore made him want to smash in the window. Before he knew it, Jesús was looking into the empty storefront. Nothing was left except the fluorescent lights and built-in bookshelves. Then he saw Mamá sweeping. Jesús banged on the door until Mamá walked over.

"What are you still doing here?" Jesús said.

The dust swirled around his mother, and Jesús sneezed.

"*Jesús te ayude,*" Mamá said.

"This place isn't ours anymore," Jesús said.

"I know, *m'ijo,*" Mamá said. "I just don't want the new people to think you're a slob."

"Let's go, Mamá."

"I'm almost done," she said.

From behind the counter she rolled out a bucket with a mop. "So," she said. "How's Don?"

"He's tired."

"And you?"

"Me too," Jesús said. "I'm tired, too."

Mamá pushed the mop across the tile to the back of the store, turned and pushed it back to Jesús' feet.

"You should've cleaned the place more," Mamá said.

"Mamá . . ."

"You're gonna live together, aren't you?"

"Yes."

"That's good," she said. Mamá wiped the sweat from the back of her neck. "He can help you with the rent."

"Don doesn't have to help me with the rent."

Mamá shook her head as she dunked the mop into the bucket. Black water squirted between her fingers as she squeezed and twisted the yarn.

"Are you so rich now that you got that insurance money?" Mamá started.

Jesús took the mop and threw it in the corner. Mamá kept looking down at the black water in the bucket.

"Don and I are leaving for a while," Jesús said.

"Where?"

"We're going to Spain."

"How . . ."

"We're just going. We need to get out of this place."

Mamá looked up at Jesús. "You're coming back, right?"

"Of course."

"Okay. Good."

The sun was setting over downtown LA.

"I'm never . . ." Jesús started saying. "You know, I'm never going to be with a woman, don't you, Mamá?"

Through the smog, he could see the Wells Fargo and Interstate buildings. Somewhere, tucked in between them, was Laemmle's cinema. Somewhere, Blondie was still bobbing up and down through aisles in busses, blowing kisses at boys.

"Mamá?"

When he turned around, Mamá was mopping again, holding on to the handle and crying.

Dark Girls

Yoli Bujanda never meant to steal. Never stole a thing, not even a pack of gum from the Woolworth's on Whittier Boulevard. Until she started her freshman year at Northwestern University, the temptation had never been there. Then she met Yasmeen Farooqi, her beautiful roommate who walked like a panther and smelled like a lily.

It all started with the boots Yasmeen had in her closet. Made in Italy, they felt like no shoe Yoli had ever felt before in her life. Maybe baby skin, but this was softer, like velvet and as fancy smelling as any perfume. She also saw other girls, rich white girls, wearing the same boots all over the campus. Yasmeen was the only dark girl she knew who owned such a baby-soft pair.

On their first day at Sargent Hall, as soon as she had unpacked her mismatched luggage, Yoli began exploring Yasmeen's closet behind a thin nylon curtain covered in daisies. The first thing Yoli saw was that pair of light brown boots, the kind she had seen horseback riders wearing on TV. The first time she touched them, she knew she was peeking into the velvet life wrapped around Yasmeen. Unzipping the side of the left boot, Yoli took off her shoe and stepped into the boot. It was a little big, but she liked the way her foot looked, tough and rich. Quickly, she put on the other boot and lay down on the bed, turned on her headphones and dozed until a voice woke her. Through her sleepy haze, she saw a dark-skinned woman leaning over her. Another woman, much older than the first, looked down on her with soft dark eyes. Yoli's stomach sank.

"Mom?"

Both women looked at each other, then laughed.

"I'm Yasmeen," the younger woman said. "You're Yolanda?"

"Yoli. Call me Yoli."

Yasmeen nodded and introduced her mother, Mrs. Farooqi, who sparkled with gold necklaces and bracelets. Yoli sat up, slowly curling her legs under her. The Farooqis were from Ridgewood, New Jersey, and they still hadn't noticed the boots on her feet.

"The safest city in the country according to President Reagan," Mrs. Farooqi said, stroking Yasmeen's hair.

Yoli smiled and rubbed the toe of the boot. Its softness helped her feel less shrunken in front of these tall dark women who dressed in gold and smelled like flowers.

I'm from East LA, she thought, one of the most danger-ous neighborhoods in Los Angeles, according to the FBI. My mother smells like Jergens cream and dresses in smocks and polyester pants. Sometimes she wears thin gold necklaces and a bracelet. I wear neither.

"I'm from Los Angeles," Yoli said.

"Oh, yes," Mrs. Farooqi said, looking serious. "But where are your parents from?"

Wasn't it obvious from the name Bujanda written in big, black marker on the purple construction paper stuck on the door? Yoli breathed in the heavy, humid air hanging in the room and mumbled, "Mexico."

Her teeth felt sore as she stared back at them. For the first time, she saw the acne scars pitting Yasmeen's face. From far away she had looked like she had fashion supermodel skin.

"Mom, let her finish napping," Yasmeen said, taking Mrs. Farooqi's arm. "We'll be back after dinner."

And then, they walked out the door.

Yoli jumped out of bed and pulled off the boots. Sweeping aside her own closet curtain, she folded the boots and hid them on the shelf above her clothes.

Outside, she heard the hallway door open, and Yasmeen and her mother returned to the room. Yoli smiled, her teeth like little knives, when they asked her to go to dinner with them.

❦ ❦

"I like your skin," Mrs. Farooqi said, looking at Yoli in the rearview as they drove down Sheridan Road to the Orrington Hotel for dinner.

Yoli nodded. She had been enjoying the air conditioning up until Mrs. Farooqi's remark. Yasmeen's unblinking profile froze facing the window.

"Yasmeen's too dark," Mrs. Farooqi continued. "How do you keep your skin so clear?"

"Noxzema," Yoli said, stroking the cream-colored leather seats that felt like Yasmeen's boots.

In the glow of the oncoming car lights, Yasmeen's hair gleamed reddish-brown. Yoli sunk her nails into the leather, hoping to puncture it, remembering the time her father ripped the braids out of her hair for looking like an *india*, when all she was trying to do was make herself look like the girl from *Little House on the Prairie*. Her fourth-grade teacher had been reading the book to her class, and she loved the way

Laura Ingalls ran around outsmarting her nemesis, Nelly Olsen. In the middle of her father's yelling and slapping, she had peed on the floor. It not only got him to stop, but it also scared him, and he never bothered her again about her braids. If only she could do that again, right there on the seat, feel the warmth just seep through her pants and spread out, tinging everything yellow.

When they arrived at the Hotel Orrington, Yoli wished she had pissed in the car. The Huddle restaurant looked nothing like the elegant exterior of the hotel. From the imitation oil lamps to the fringed velvet canopies hanging over the booths, the whole place felt like it would fall apart the moment they sat down.

"Order anything you want," Mrs. Farooqi said. "My treat."

"We should have gone into Chicago," Yasmeen said, picking up a menu.

"We are in Chicago," Mrs. Farooqi said.

"This is Evanston."

"Oh, it's close enough."

When the waiter came and took their order, Mrs. Farooqi asked Yoli why she had ordered her hamburger rare. Yoli told her that's how her mother cooked all their burgers, but really, she had learned to order meat from the actress playing Joan Crawford in a movie called *Mommie Dearest*. "That's the only way to eat steak," Joan had told her daughter, who refused to eat the bloody piece of meat. No matter that Joan Crawford was a bitch in the movie, Yoli liked the idea of blood on a plate.

Yoli could not wait to rip into that hamburger when their orders arrived. That way, she wouldn't have to answer more of Yasmeen and Mrs. Farooqi's questions until she finished eating. She could always give better answers on a full stomach.

Yoli hadn't eaten since her lunch on the airplane seven hours earlier, but refused to gobble down the hard, cold bread rolls. Instead, she drank the ice water and crunched the ice with her teeth. The combination of ice and hunger froze her. Already, she could feel the winter coming on, despite the humidity and lush green she saw out the windows.

For the first time in her life, Yoli craved a bowl of her mother's steaming hot meatball soup. Up until this dinner, she thought she was done with Mexican food. The thought of those big, juicy *albóndigas* floating in a steaming broth of onions and carrots made her stomach feel flat and empty. She knew then that she'd be hungry and cold at Northwestern, no matter how much bloody meat she ate.

"So what will you study while you're here?" Mrs. Farooqi asked.

"English," Yoli said and drank more water.

"I'm pre-med," Yasmeen said.

"I don't like reading," Mrs. Farooqi said. "But I admire writers."

Yasmeen looked around. "Here comes our food," she said as the waitress carried the plates out to the table.

"Couldn't you have studied English in California?" Mrs. Farooqi asked, smiling as the waitress set their plates in front of them. Red oily juice seeped out of Yoli's burger onto the white plate.

"I wanted to get away from my family," Yoli answered before lifting the burger to her mouth, trying to hide behind it before taking a wide deep bite.

Yasmeen laughed. Mrs. Farooqi kept smiling as she swirled her pasta noodles around her fork.

"Wanted to get as far away as possible," Yoli said, readying herself for another bite. "They drive me nuts."

Yasmeen looked down into her chicken sandwich while munching on its side of fries. When she asked Yoli if she was going home to Los Angeles for the winter break, Yoli nodded, even though she hadn't thought about it.

"I'm sure your family misses you," Mrs. Farooqi said and reached for Yasmeen, who took her jeweled hand in hers.

While they were looking at each other like lovers, Yoli took the saltshaker with the words "The Huddle" printed on it and threw it into her purse. She kept nodding, biting and chewing until nothing was left on her plate but bloody juice.

❧⁓❧

Mrs. Farooqi left for New Jersey the next day, never noticing Yasmeen's missing boots and thinking Yoli would get along with her daughter. And Yoli did, until November when Greg Strik, another student who lived in Bobb-McCulloch Hall, came along and started dating Yasmeen. Great, Yoli thought. First, Yasmeen's mother grilled her like she didn't belong at the school, now Yasmeen had stolen the cutest guy she had ever met in her life. Why hadn't he asked her out? After all, just like her, he was a cafeteria worker. And just like her, he was getting through school on loans, scholarships and dishwashing. Sometimes they both worked the food line during Sunday brunch, but the rest of the week they washed dishes, unloaded trays and wiped slimy meat out of the garbage disposal. During lulls between trays of dirty dishes and glasses, they'd bitch about the rich students who didn't have to do shitty jobs like dishwashing and slopping out food.

"It's their world," Greg said, snapping food down the disposal. "We're just here to clean up."

When he said that, Yoli knew she could love him. She really started to fall in love when she dropped a tray full of danishes on the floor and Greg came scurrying over to help. Not only did he help her pick them up, but instead of throwing them away, he placed the danishes on the fancy plastic tray made to look like cut glass. Greg smiled at her. Yoli laughed and put the tray in the refrigerated case.

Every time they saw a student biting into one, they shook their heads and laughed. After work, Yoli asked Greg if he wanted to study with her and Yasmeen at Mudd Library. When he said yes, she couldn't believe her luck. And when he told her he had records and tapes by New Order, Joy Division and the Sugar Cubes, she fell in love completely.

How was she to know that he would find dark, pimply Yasmeen attractive? Yoli's second mistake was leaving them alone together too long when she wandered around the stacks or sank her laundry quarters down a vending machine for chocolate bars. When he walked them back to their dorm room, Yoli's heart thumped hard enough to rip through her throat. One night, just after Greg had left them, Yasmeen grew quiet. She quickly changed into her pajamas and went out to the bathroom to brush her teeth and wash her face. After a minute sitting on her bed, Yoli went to her closet, pulled out Yasmeen's boots and put them on. She lay down on her bed, admiring those boots until she heard Yasmeen walking back down the hallway. Zip, zip, she peeled them off and slid them deep under her bed. Yasmeen asked her something when she came in.

"Looking for my slippers," Yoli said, sitting up.

"What?" Yasmeen said bending down to Yoli's face. "I have to ask you something."

"What?"

"You like Greg, don't you?"

"He looks like Bernard Sumner."

"Who?"

"Lead singer for New Order."

"He's very nice, I think."

"Yes, he is. I'd go crazy without him at work."

Yasmeen stood up and nodded, wiping her face with her hand towel, then climbed into bed. The next day, Yoli woke up earlier than usual for her brunch shift at the cafeteria. For three hours straight, she scrambled and served eggs. Students didn't even bother to smile or nod at Yoli. They just looked at the food. But it didn't matter because she knew Greg would ask her out that day.

Later, when Greg walked Yoli back to her room, he asked Yasmeen out. It happened just before they were about to head out for Mudd Library, while Yoli went quickly to the bathroom. As Yoli and Greg walked the winding path beside Lake Michigan, he told her Yasmeen had said yes to him. Suddenly the trees reached down and slapped their bare branches against her face. She tried to push through, but everything sounded muffled. Lake Michigan glittered under the full moon, bright and beautiful. He was taking Yasmeen to the Orrington, to The Huddle. Of course. Yoli kept walking, staring straight ahead, afraid she would start yelling or crying. They walked through the library's revolving doors and down the stairs to the check-in desk. She'd forgotten her student ID card. Greg asked to let Yoli through, but the kid at the desk shook her head.

"I'll meet you at our usual spot," Greg told her.

Yoli never went back, her heart an open cut.

When she got back to the dorm room, all she could think about was Greg and how he didn't want her. She pulled out the boots from under the bed, put them on and walked over to the shore of Lake Michigan. As she climbed down to one of the large rocks she liked to sit on, she cried silently. Once she got to her favorite spot, she sat down, wrapped her arms around her knees and began stroking her boots, reminding herself that her skin was smoother and clearer.

⛬

Yasmeen was on the rag again. Yoli could tell. She had been watching Yasmeen more closely lately, studying her, trying to pick up her ways to understand why Greg would want such a dark, pitted girl who only opened her mouth to say "yes" or "no." There were little rolled up pieces of tissue paper flecked with red in her wastebasket. They looked like little polka-dotted tissue eggs. Tampons, she thought. Yoli's mother never allowed her to use tampons when she first got her period.

"Only married women use those," she told Yoli when she brought it up.

For a while she believed her mother. None of her high school friends used them. In college, tampons were all that the girls used.

"You still wear those?" Yasmeen asked her one day after Yoli got back from the drugstore. She had just pulled out the box of Always with wings and was tucking them deep into her closet.

"Haven't worn those since I was 13," Yasmeen said. "Did they run out of tampons?"

"Don't they hurt?" Yoli asked.

"No," she said, laughing. "You just have to put them in right."

So when Yoli started using them, she had the hardest time making sure they were deep inside and wouldn't slip out when she started walking. Otherwise, if they poked out a teeny little bit, it would hurt just to sit down. When she got her period over winter break, her mother came in with a tissue egg hanging from her pinched thumb and forefinger.

"*¿Qué's esto?*" Mom asked.

Yoli's skin chilled and her head throbbed with heat.

"Is this what we send you to college for? To learn about these things?" her mother said.

"All the girls use them."

"Your father saw these things and thought someone was bleeding to death."

Yoli almost laughed.

"Don't let him know," her mother said. "It'll kill him."

As soon as her mother left, Yoli walked down to Johnson's Market and bought a box of Always feminine napkins. She laughed a little at the way the old lady cashier double-wrapped the box in pink plastic bags like the napkins would bleed through the box.

Once she got back to Northwestern after the break, Yoli spent a chunk of her loan money on a long black 100-percent wool coat, the kind Yasmeen and every other student wore at that school. And she stocked up on tampons, stuffing them under her bed until there were about a dozen boxes.

"I need to talk to you," Yasmeen said from her desk.

"Shouldn't you be in class?" Yoli said. She thought she had timed it to be alone in the dorm room while she brought in the boxes.

"Look," Yasmeen said, grabbing the boots out of Yoli's closet. "I know you took these from me."

Yoli froze and looked up at her.

"Greg's in love with me, you know," Yasmeen said.

Before Yoli knew it, her anger gushed out of her like blood. "Don't know why," Yoli said. "You're ugly and dark, just like your mother said."

Yasmeen looked ready to scream or cry. Yoli couldn't tell. She waited for Yasmeen to call her a name, hit her, do something any other person from East LA would do. Instead, Yasmeen dropped her boots, quickly put on her coat and walked out the door.

Yoli grabbed her new coat and wrapped her scarf around her neck, chin and nose. When she stepped out onto the campus, she saw Yasmeen, a dark silhouette in the snow, headed toward Bobb-McCulloch, toward Greg. The building's buff brick glowed yellow in the whiteness. Black, dead vines strangled the limestone bricks. The lake wind cut through Yoli's coat as she tried to keep up with Yasmeen. The snow's brightness blinded her even though the sky was overcast. She should have taken Yasmeen's sunglasses while she was at it. Everything was cold and had been cold ever since she had come to this school.

"Lake effect," somebody had told her. Had it been Greg or one of her professors?

"Whatever it is, this place is always cold," she muttered as she kept walking, sinking her face deeper into her scarf.

She stopped suddenly when she saw Yasmeen meet up with Greg on the pathway. He took her hand and walked toward one of the fraternity houses, probably one of the many he was rushing to impress Yasmeen.

"Sellout," Yoli whispered as she kept walking toward Bobb-McCulloch. She still needed to know why he loved Yasmeen, and the answer was in Greg's room. She knew this. Yoli stood at the entrance and waited for someone to walk out. As she followed a student to the stairwell, she felt like she was floating. Greg's door was open. Yasmeen used to do the same with their door until she practically moved in with Greg. Yoli looked around.

On his walls were the latest posters for New Order's *Brotherhood* album and another for the Depeche Mode's *Music for the Masses*. When she saw a bottle of Yasmeen's Eternity perfume on Greg's dresser, she knew he had sold out completely. Her palms hummed as she slipped it into her coat pocket. As she walked around looking for more of Yasmeen's things, she started floating again. In Greg's closet she found rows of high heels, soft leather flats and pumps. A pair of black riding boots lay deep in the back of the closet. But they didn't tempt her. No, not like the first pair. Yoli whipped around when she saw something red out the corner of her eye. It was a cutesy red metal trash can with gold flowers and vines wrapping around it. Yasmeen's for sure.

Yoli knelt down and sifted through the trash with both hands, looking closely at each torn piece of paper. She smoothed out a crumpled piece of paper that turned out to be a letter with Northwestern letterhead stating that Yasmeen was on academic probation. Blood rushed to Yoli's face. This was it, she thought. This was it. As she walked out, she kept smoothing the letter against her coat and did not notice the cleaning lady with her equipment.

"What are you doing here?" the lady asked.

"Nothing," Yoli said.

"Give me that," the lady said, holding out a chapped brown hand.

"It's my friend Yasmeen's," Yoli blurted out and took off running down the stairs, through the front door and across the quad.

Somewhere in between Bobb-McCulloch Hall and Delta Tau Delta she dropped Yasmeen's letter in the snow.

The humid June air weighed on Yoli as she stripped her New Order posters from the cinder block walls of her room, balled them up and threw them out the window. Occasionally a breeze rippled the tree leaves and water on the lake but never made it into the dorm room. Everything had turned green almost overnight. Flowers, trees and grass had sprung up all at once, when only a few days earlier everything had seemed bare and brown.

Yasmeen was at her desk, cleaning out her drawers and packing her books. The bareness of the white room made Yoli feel smaller, browner than on the first day she had arrived. She turned up the OMD song on her Walkman to fill the silence and push out the memory of the cleaning woman's chapped hand. Still, the woman hadn't stopped Yoli from making one more trip to Greg's room, where she found Yasmeen's letter from a New York state school sitting on his desk. She thought for sure that Greg would break up the relationship, now that Yasmeen had to transfer to an easy state school. So when Greg walked into their room with a box of Yasmeen's things, Yoli watched him expectantly.

"Mom will be here soon," Yasmeen said to Greg. "You better go."

She kissed Greg on the lips, then held him as if she would never let him go. Yoli suddenly felt a cold piercing pain shoot through her chest. She remained at her desk, staring out the window at the windsurfers with their brightly colored sails.

"Goodbye, Yoli," he said, waving.

"Goodbye."

After he left, Yasmeen returned to her packing. Yoli stroked Yasmeen's boots, which she had worn to help her get through seeing Greg and Yasmeen together. Yoli could feel her legs beginning to sweat.

"My mother doesn't know about Greg," she said, looking like she was about to cry. "Please don't tell her."

"Is he going with you?" Yoli asked, hoping he wouldn't.

Yasmeen shook her head. She added that he would drive to Ridgewood and stay at a motel close to her parents' house for a while. Another cold pain shot through Yoli. It didn't matter to Greg that Yasmeen liked that Motown crap Chicago radios played. Didn't matter at all that she was darker, scarred and a dropout. Greg loved her. But Northwestern didn't. Of course, it didn't love Yoli either, but at least she hadn't flunked out. At least she would still be here next year.

Mrs. Farooqi arrived, dressed in gold like that first day. Yoli nodded and smiled as she turned to face her. Mrs. Farooqi put her hand on Yasmeen's face and whispered something that made Yasmeen stiffen.

"For these last few days, can you just leave me alone?" Yasmeen challenged her mother.

Mrs. Farooqi's eyes widened. She stepped back, then turned to Yoli. Her eyes shifted downward to Yoli's legs and feet.

"Those are Yasmeen's?" Mrs. Farooqi asked.

Yoli pulled her legs up onto her chair and wrapped her arms around them. The boots felt hotter than ever, but she wasn't going to take them off.

"Did you give those to her?" Mrs. Farooqi asked Yasmeen, who just kept packing.

"I gave them to her," Yasmeen said. "Leave her alone."

Yoli heard Mrs. Farooqi say something in Farsi and then the word "expensive." They argued a little, but Yasmeen seemed to win out. Yoli felt like telling Mrs. Farooqi about Greg and then throwing the damn boots at her. She felt like grabbing hold of her hair, the way girls at her high school did when they got into fights in the bathrooms and slammed each other's faces into the tiled floors. Instead, Yoli unzipped the boots, gently folded them and placed them on Yasmeen's desk. Then she pulled out the bottle of Eternity perfume from her dresser and put it on top of the boots. Both women said nothing as Yoli walked barefoot out into the hallway and out of Sargent Hall.

As she made her way to the lakeshore, walking the asphalted path through the Sports Pavilion parking lot, Yoli kept saying, "I'm here. I'm still here." Over and over she said that until she was ankle-deep in the cold lake water and her legs had cooled off.

Happiness Is Right Next to You

———

When my regular hairdresser, Beto, can't get me an appointment during the winter break, I go back to César's Palace on Whittier Boulevard for my hair cut. Mango isn't there anymore, but there's this new girl, Josie. I hope to God she's better than Mango because I have to look good for Luly Valdez's wedding.

When I step into a mist of Aqua Net and acetone, Josie makes me sit at her station. She pulls my hair strands, then scrunches them. My curly fried hair looks especially dry under the fluorescent lights of the salon. Before Josie can ask me what I want, I tell her to bob it.

"*¿Todo?*" she asks, fanning her red nails through my frizzy ringlets.

"Yes, all of it," I declare.

Luly is the first one in our circle of friends to get married. She's tying the knot with this Chicano guy she met at UCLA while studying for her BA in English. Jorge, or George, as I used to call him when we went to Griffith Junior High School, is the same guy who dumped me back then for Yoli Macías, a blonde with big boobs.

Josie leads me to the shampoo station and leans me back over the sink.

"I love weddings," Josie says as she shampoos my hair, digging her nails into my scalp.

"I don't."

Josie smirks. Her nails cut deeper into my head.

"When you get married . . ." she starts.

I close my eyes and drift off, thinking about the lousy haircut Mango gave me when I was fourteen and my promise to myself to never do another cheap haircut in East LA. My heart beats quickly at the thought of the lopsided feathered hair that left my left ear poking out of the uneven strands.

"Is Luly your sister?" Josie asks.

"She's my friend. We both go to UCLA."

"That's nice," Josie says. "Is that where she met her fiancé?"

"Yeah. His name is Jorge. I knew him in junior high school."

I don't tell her that Jorge used to be my boyfriend. Warm water rinses my head, lulls me into a little nap before Josie speaks again.

"The wedding theme is 'Happiness Is Right Next to You,'" I tell her. Instantly, I regret it.

"You have to fit the theme," Josie says, sitting me up and walking me to her station. My hair drips. "Happiness is good. So are weddings."

"*Puro pedo*, bullshit," I can hear my abuela Merced say. My *tía* Suki would laugh and say, "Happiness is only on TV and in the movies . . . and only happens to rich people. When it's poor people, it's only because they marry rich people."

"How short?" Josie asks, stretching my hair to make it longer.

"Cut it up to here," I say, placing my hand up to my cheekbone.

Josie's forehead scrunches. I am so ready for that look, the but-men-really-like-long-hair-and-how-are-you-gonna-find-your-own-happiness-if-you-cut-off-all-your-hair-look. My longtime hairdresser Beto would have refused, but Josie has to do it.

Josie proceeds to pull out the drawer filled with scissors and plastic rat tail combs.

I rub my eyes. My contacts are killing me, but I want to make sure I can see how this chick cuts my hair. Wet chunks of hair hit my nose and cheeks as the scissor blades grind against each other.

Soon Josie opens another drawer, this one filled with round brushes. She takes the second-fattest one and wraps a side section of my hair around it, pulling it straight towards her. She gets into a rhythm. Like Mango, she lets the heat from the blow dryer burn my scalp, but I say nothing. It feels good to hurt. When Josie's done, my hair looks soft and shiny, like a wig, but a nice expensive one.

"Looks good," Josie says. "Good hair."

"Happy hair," I laugh.

Underneath my chair, black clumps float around the floor. One of the other hairdressers walks by pushing my newly chopped strands with a broom. It took me years to grow it down to my waist, and now it's gone. I remember when Jorge used to wrap it around his fingers and pull it over his face while we lay on Merced's couch.

"Don't ever cut your hair," he said then.

And for a long time after junior high school, I never cut it, hoping it would bring him back to me. I even fried it into spiral curls like Luly's hair, but he never even called me.

"You look ready for the wedding," Josie says.

I'm ready for happiness. I think.

⮞⮜

"But money can't buy happiness," my friend Terry tells me. We're driving down I-10 toward Beverly Hills, toward the church.

"No," I say. "But I'd like to try."

"I can't believe he doesn't remember," Terry says, pulling at the spiral curls hanging down the sides of her face.

Josie did those this morning as a favor for me, and a promise that I would come to her for my next haircut. Terry's wearing her skin-tight red dress with a black velvet choker. She's hoping she'll be the next one to get her M-R-S degree from her white boyfriend Jason. Me? I'm going for the free booze and the DJ music. But mostly I'm going to see Jorge.

"Don't tell Luly," I say. "I'm only telling you because I'm leaving right after they get married."

I decided that this morning, while I was wiping on my foundation.

Terry grabs my right arm. "Luly's still going to want to see you."

More guilt. But for my own peace of mind, I know I have to leave. It's either that or get so drunk I black out the images of Luly and Jorge kissing at the altar, dancing their first dance together, eating together, everything together. I know Luly will ask for me. I know Jorge's mom will wonder about me. But they'll soon forget, just like Jorge.

"You have to stay," Terry says. "I don't want to sit by myself."

I grip the steering wheel. I feel so stupid. Why did I even accept the invitation? I turn on the radio and "I Go Crazy" croons over the speakers.

"My heart just can't hide," Paul Davis sings. I turn down the radio.

"Really?" I say more to the music than to Terry. "Why didn't Jason come with you?"

"You know why," she says.

Because Jason's watching another college basketball game. It's "March Madness," which includes the fans and players. Personally, I think Jason just doesn't want to stay with Terry. She's too Mexican for him and his WASP family living in Orange County. As we get closer to the church, my armpits start sweating. My red velvet dress and silk shawl are too thick for a spring wedding but they're the only decent things I have. Besides, Cher wore the same dress in the movie, *Moonstruck*. It's perfect for winter in New York but not for a warm spring in LA. It cost me my semester's tuition and it looks good. I need to look good today. I need to look better than Luly.

"Maybe I'll stay," I tell Terry as we walk up the cement steps to the Beverly Hills Presbyterian Church which, except for the bell tower, looks like the gym building at my junior high school. White paint and delicate thin bars cover the windows. Inside, the dark wood glows warm with the tapered candles. No saints, no gory Jesus hanging bloody from a huge wooden cross. Definitely not Catholic. I wonder if Luly's mom approves. If she's like other Mexican mothers, she believes that the only real marriages happen at a Catholic church. Where are the *mariachis?* Every Mamá, even my own, loves a good torchy *mariachi* song.

I pull my shawl tighter around my bare shoulders. Even though I'm an atheist, I still feel Jesus looking at me, bringing down the giant wooden cross with him like a Catholic superman. The silk tightens around me. Then I see her. Yolanda Macías, the one Jorge dumped me for while we were still dating. All of my junior high school heartbreak starts crackling inside of me. I'm craving a shot of brandy, the kind my grandmother drinks when she thinks of her long-lost love. Yolie stands next to a short Mexican guy, her brother Art. He's wearing a shiny blue suit, wet around the collar from the sweat rolling down the back of his head.

Yolie looks fatter, especially in her shantung silk yellow pantsuit, and her long blond hair hangs limply at the waist. My head feels suddenly light with my new bob. As we walk down the aisle, my heels click on the tile. With every step, the tight leather pumps pinch my toes. When I bought them, I was so sure the suede would feel soft inside as well as out. Obviously, I fucked up. Already, I can feel a blister popping on top of my pinky toe.

"You know Jorge?" Luly asked me the first time we all met up at a college club mixer.

"A little," I said, looking straight at Jorge.

Jorge looked exactly the same with his golden-brown hair and pale, pimpled face. His eyes still had that marble shine. The only difference was that he was wider at the shoulders. After a few wine coolers, I sat down right next to him. I nodded at him.

Jorge gave me this confused look, tilted his head to one side like he really couldn't figure me out.

My heart cracked, and I sipped my wine cooler, looked down at my thighs, the same ones he used to squeeze when we were at the movies or at Merced's house watching TV.

"How'd you meet Luly?" I asked.

"Economics class," he said. "She sat up front, next to me."

It made sense. Guys were always after Luly. She was blonde and fair skinned. Thin too. Of course, she would be the first one to get a boyfriend, to get married.

All the pews are packed. Near the end of the aisle, Terry finds a spot right close to the altar, right behind Jorge's mom. I want to sit on Luly's side, but there's no room. Mrs. Zamudio recognizes me right away.

"Lucha!" she says. "You cut your hair."

I nod. She looks exactly the same with her big cartoon eyes. Instead of a bouffant style, her hair is cut short, permed out with fuchsia red highlights. Her frosted lips shine under the sunlight burning through the stained-glass windows. Even now, on her son's wedding day, she still wears big fake eyelashes. Terry goes up to her, kisses each of her cheeks, leaving red lip marks. Mrs. Zamudio holds out her arms. The moment I hug her, I start to cry and hang on to her like she's a rock.

"It's okay," she says, squeezing me. "It's okay."

When I hear the *mariachis*, I know I have to stop. I put my hands over my eyes. I just can't watch Luly walking down the aisle. Terry pulls me down next to her.

"Jorge saw you," she says. "He saw the whole thing."

I don't care. I just wipe my eyes and look at his profile. Finally, Jorge looks at me.

I mouth, "I still love you."

Peroxide

Armida used to roll up her hair like Jean Harlow. Or at least she thought it looked like the actress' platinum blonde hair. But instead of being real smooth on the top, tiny hairs would stick out and all the little pin curls would fall weak and straight. Poor thing. She tried, but what can you do with hair like an *india*? Too black. Too rough. And the look back in the 1930s, Harlowe's time, was like smooth and gold.

Armida had nice thin eyebrows that she did not draw in with pencil. No, she just plucked them so thin, like all the artists used to do back then. Her face was perfect—except that it was a little too dark and her nose was a little too round. She had a cute little mole just above her lip, which was plucked and mustache-free. She was so taken with movie stars that she made her husband Enrique and their five kids move out to LA from Arizona. At least, that's what she told me.

"Look what I made," she said one time, showing me a necklace made with little flower buttons that looked like daisies with earrings to match. "Don't I look like Harlowe?"

Pobrecita Armida. No Harlowe there, not with that burlap sack dress and huaraches. She looked more like some crazy Apache in one of those Tom Mix movies. I think she was bored with Enrique and taking care of their kids. Every time I visited her little bungalow next door, the babies were naked.

"*Por Dios*, Armida," I'd tell her. "Put some diapers on those kids. They're peeing all over the place."

Armida would just laugh. "Oh, they're fine. . . . Don't worry about it."

One time, she showed me the latest photo of some movie starlet and asked me if she should dye her hair blonde.

"I bought some bottles of peroxide at the Woolworth's," she said. "I read in *Screen Album* that all the movie stars are doing this now. Just pour a bottle over the head and, *tan tan,* platinum blonde."

"Not Dolores del Río," I said.

"*Ay*, that's why you hardly see her in the movies anymore."

Armida flipped through the pages and showed me all the photos. She was right. Greta Garbo, Lana Turner, Ginger Rogers, even Rosita Quintana . . . all blonde. Whatever happened to Dolores or Mona Maris or Joan Crawford? Everybody wanted to be a blonde in 1938. And not just *rubia* but super white blonde.

Just imagine, a little dark thing with feet like tortillas and skin like a clay bowl with blonde hair? *Qué horror.*

She wasn't the only one dying her hair, hoping to look whiter. Some of my *comadres* were experimenting with the peroxide, their hair often coming out orangey, never really blonde. The only way you were gonna get a Jean Harlow look was to go to César's Salon and pay a lot of cash for it. No matter, even after investing in the classy dye job, they never really looked like Harlowe. They were just *indias* with blonde hair.

"Save your money for the kids," I said.

Armida looked over at her daughter Mari, who was playing with her little rag doll, and laughed. "Oh, they don't need anything."

"Clothes for school?" I said, looking at her other daughter, Clara, in the faded blue dress she wore almost every day.

"Don't be silly, Lorena," she said. "They don't care about clothes at their age. They just need to learn."

I walked over to her bedroom and saw the baby naked and peeing on her bed.

"*Mira*, how cute," Armida said, pointing to his little penis as it squirted. "It's like a fountain."

Then she called me over to the bathroom and showed me a couple of big bottles of peroxide.

"All I have to do is drench your hair, rinse and you will look like . . . Who's your favorite blonde?"

I was too busy trying to put a diaper on baby Enrique and, before I could stop myself, I said, "Lana Turner."

She handed me the bottle and said, "You can be Lana, but you'll have to pluck your eyebrows first."

As Armida returned the bottles of peroxide to the cabinet under the bathroom sink, she said, "They were on sale, but don't tell Enrique." She hugged me close and whispered, "Just between us girls."

Qué loca. How was she going to hide her head from her husband when he came back from the mines? She was lucky Enrique worked in Arizona instead of California. Personally, I think he had another honey on the side, but I never said anything to Armida. What else would keep him away from his own kids? So maybe her hair would grow back to its natural color by the time he came back in December.

Ay, these new women . . . they were born here, so they had all these crazy ideas about being independent instead of taking care of their families. "*Pachucas*," they called themselves, but they looked more like sluts, wearing their short, tight skirts and shaving their eyebrows. With their hair piled high . . . no wonder people thought they hid razor blades in it.

Armida had this one friend, Fifi, but if she was French, I was Lana Turner. She started going over to Armida's house a lot and playing some crazy music I could hear through the kitchen window.

"Boogie-woogie," Armida called it, when I asked her about it later.

The fake Frenchy's hair was that peroxide orange and showed her roots. So I knew then where Armida was getting her stupid ideas.

One afternoon, little Imelda came in dancing a crazy dance.

"Jitterbug," Fifi laughed. "Jitterbug," she repeated as she started dancing, throwing Imelda around like a sack.

I never heard Imelda laugh and scream so hard. It looked so dangerous, I was afraid Imelda would go flying out the window. I rubbed my eyebrows. Maybe while the kids slept I would have time to fix them.

"I'm taking the kids again?" I said. I reached for Imelda's hand, but she just kept dancing that jitterbug with Fifi.

"We're going to see *Ninotchka* at El Capitán," Armida said. "I'll pay you back. Honest."

I took the kids to their rooms and didn't even think again about my eyebrows that night.

❧ ❧

"You have to do this, Lorena," Armida said. "Do it with me."

"Are you crazy?" I said. "Mando would kill me."

"No, he wouldn't," she said. "Don't you always catch him looking at that waitress who lives down the street? She's a blonde. He'll love it."

"Not if it comes out orange. Why don't you get your friend Fifi to do it?"

"She doesn't like that platinum shade."

So, and this is how dumb I was, I let her pour the bottle over my head. Even after I could smell my hair kind of burning, I let her keep pouring. Then she dipped my head into the bathroom sink, almost hitting it on the faucet when she ran the cold water over me.

"Let's wrap your head in a towel for a little while because it's supposed to stay warm in order to take hold."

Well, I should've let her do it to her hair first before I let her touch mine. Armida looked like she was about to cry when she saw how my hair came out. I just wanted to kill her.

"But I did what the magazine said," she said, wiping her eyes.

"What *pinche* magazine?"

And she pulled out *The Ladies Companion* magazine and showed me these pictures of blonde after blonde. They even had "before" and "after" pictures, but I noticed none of the models were *indias* like us.

"All these women . . . ," I said. "Look at that 'before' hair. It's soft and light."

I threw the towel over my head and ran back to my bungalow. No matter how much I shampooed it, my hair glowed red-orange like a lit match tip. I could've lived with it if only my hair hadn't started drying out. Mando laughed so hard when he came home from work.

"That's what you get for listening to that crazy *vieja*," he said.

He was right. Why had I listened to her? I should've known better because, really, she didn't even know how to read. She just looked at the pictures of a woman pouring something out of a brown bottle over a woman's head. No water or conditioner or anything. And Mando was not going to let me live this down until the day he died.

"You're just as bad as she is," he said. "I look more like Jean Harlow than both of you together."

From then on, I stopped taking care of her kids.

"Armida," I told her through my bedroom window, "I'm not going out of this house until my hair comes back."

"*Ay, Dios,*" she said, "can you still watch the kids?"

"No, I can't," I said. "You should stay home and stop going to the movies so much."

And that was that.

I'd sit at my window and sometimes see Armida going out with Fifi to the movies and leaving her oldest to take care of the kids. I felt so bad for them, but Armida had to learn her lesson. One time, I noticed Armida had been gone for almost the whole weekend. Nobody came in or out of her house. I thought she must have taken her kids because I didn't see Clara or Imelda come out to play. Fifi came by and knocked on Armida's door.

When she saw me, she ran up to my window. "Have you seen my *carnala*?" she asked.

"No, I haven't seen her in three days."

Her eyes looked like witch's eyes, with all that eyeliner and eyeshadow. "Did she take the kids with her?"

"I think so. . . . I haven't seen any of them."

"*Cabrona,*" she cursed Armida and went back to her front door and started pounding on it. "Armida! Imelda! Clara! Open the fucking door!"

After kicking the door with her peek-a-boo shoes, Fifi threw a shoe at the door and then sat down on the steps. When she saw me again, she ran over to my window.

"Can you give me a ride somewhere?"

She was panting like a dog, and her make-up was running down her cheeks. She looked more like a little girl instead of a tough *pachuca.*

"No," I said. "I don't have a car."

She wiped her face with her hands, which was a mistake because now that cheap eyeliner was really making her cry.

"I need to get to El Capitán now," she said. "Fuckin' Armida." She started walking down the street. I never saw her again.

⁓

Later that night, I heard Armida come back. I stayed awake until I heard her turn off the radio.

"Probably has another guy," Mando said while I warmed up tortillas for him the next morning.

I could hear her crazy music coming through the window. But something was missing.

"I don't hear the kids running around screaming," Mando said.

After Mando left for work, I went over to her house. For some reason, I started to feel really sad as I stood on the porch and knocked on the door. Maybe it was because I saw Imelda's little doll on the floor. It looked so dirty and lonely.

Armida opened the door. I don't know how she did it, and instead of an *india* with orange hair, it was an *india* with Jean Harlow hair. She had shaved her eyebrows and drew them with an eyebrow pencil.

"I look like her, don't I?" was the first thing she said to me, standing there fluffing up her hair. That was no bottled peroxide job. That was professional.

"It's real good," I said, "real good. How much did you pay?"

She put her hand to her heart, romantic-like. Then I noticed the dress. A nice blue cotton with a lace collar. Definitely not homemade.

"I used the Woolworth's bottle, Lorena," she said. "What do you think?"

Bullshit. Then I saw Mari behind her, without diapers of course, with little Enrique Jr.'s toy bird.

"Where's Enrique?" I asked her. "Where have you been all these days?"

She couldn't even look me in the eye. "With his grandmother," she said.

"In Arizona?" I asked.

"Yeah. What? Can't I have a little vacation?"

"But who took him there?"

Then I noticed that Imelda wasn't running around the living room like she did in the mornings.

"Clara and Imelda are down there too," Armida said. "*¡Chingado,* Lorena! Can't I have a *pinche* break once in a while?"

She turned away from me and looked in the mirror by the front door, twisting a blonde curl around her finger. I didn't even ask about Mima.

"Fifi was looking for you," I said.

Armida kept twisting her curl as she headed for her bedroom.

"Did you see her?" I asked. "She said something about going to El Capitán to find you."

"She was too late."

Then she pulled out a suitcase and started packing.

"Where are you going?" I asked.

"You don't understand, Lorena. You have it easy."

I didn't know what in hell she was talking about. She seemed to be the one with the easy life, now that she just had one kid to take care of.

"How could you . . ." but I couldn't finish.

Armida kept packing, then took off her slippers and went into her closet. She pulled out some peek-a-boo shoes and then put on a nice, new wool coat.

"Tell Enrique, Mari and I went back to Durango. No. Tell him you don't know where we went."

I just sat down on the bed and watched her pack, admiring her hair but hating her hands. I never noticed how small and smooth they were. Mine looked like brown chicken claws.

"I have to go," I said.

Armida just kept looking at herself in the mirror and adjusting her hat. "Okay," she said but didn't look at me.

I walked back to my house and turned on the radio. Lalo Guerrero was singing "Pachuco Boogie," the same song that Imelda and Fifi danced to that day Armida went to see that Garbo movie. From my window, I watched Armida walk down to Whittier Boulevard the same way Fifi had done. Armida carried Mari on her hip as she loped down the street. I watched her until she turned the corner, and I kept looking until I saw the number 18 bus drive by. I thought I could see her blonde head, but it could've been another woman.

Later when Mando came home, I told him about Armida and the kids.

"Did you call the police?" he asked.

I shook my head. What for? The kids would never be found. Maybe they'd have a better life. I'll never forget Mando's stare when I told him this. It was like I was a stranger. He'd been at the kitchen table eating his *picadillo* and suddenly, he got up.

"Where are you going?" I asked.

He didn't answer. I knew he was going to the Silver Dollar Bar, where that waitress worked.

Instead of crying for hours in bed until he came back, I walked over to Armida's house and looked through her bedroom window. The bathroom light was still on. Her burlap dress was on the bed, and the pictures of her kids and Enrique were still on the wall. It looked like they were all coming back. It was like they went out to see a movie or went food shopping. When I came back home, I went into the bathroom and pulled out the last bottle of peroxide Armida had given me. I held it in my hand for a little bit, opened it and poured it down the sink.

Boulevard Saints

That Easter Sunday, Whittier Boulevard bustled with shoppers who had just attended Mass at the East LA churches: Soledad, St. Alphonsus, Our Lady of Lourdes and El Santuario de Nuestra Señora de Guadalupe. Despite the solemn holiday, the roar of the drunken gang at the Silver Dollar Bar could be heard beyond its tattered red curtains and plate glass windows. Whooping *ranchera* songs floated above the stream of families, students and shoppers. The women walked briskly, avoiding the men peering from the darkness.

At the corner of Whittier and Fetterly stood a girl holding up a cardboard poster that read, "America is a myth." Below those words was its translation: "*EUA es un mito.*" She wore her hair in braids and had a red kerchief masking her nose and mouth. She had on a T-shirt with a drawing of the Virgen de Guadalupe in a sombrero and with ammunition belts crisscrossing her chest.

Cala and her grandmother, Doña Goya, neared the girl as they walked over to Thrifty's after Mass at El Santuario.

Suddenly the old woman stopped. "*¿Qué's eso de un mito?*" Doña Goya asked her granddaughter, Cala.

"A myth, Grandma, something that's not true," Cala answered.

On closer inspection, Doña Goya noticed the image of the Virgin and said, "She has no respect."

Cala rolled her eyes. She knew her grandmother held the Virgencita in the highest esteem, even higher than Jesús Malverde, the renegade saint from Sinaloa. Today of all days, Easter Sunday, Cala felt the disrespect along with her grandmother. Besides Christmas, this was the day Cala wore her best dress and her polished leather pumps. Although she had shined them this morning, they were already scuffed up after climbing up the concrete stairs to El Santuario de Nuestra Señora de Guadalupe on First Street. Afterwards, they had to catch two buses to get to Thrifty's Drugstore on Whittier Boulevard.

Cala's feathered hair had already frizzed out from the heat and sweat. Her sweaty feet throbbed with each step she took on the concrete sidewalk. Her grandmother, covered in her best black *rebozo* and orange flowery cotton dress, hadn't even broken a sweat.

"I still don't understand why you wanted to come all the way down here," her grandmother said. "We could have had *raspados* at El Mercado down the street from the church."

Cala knew her high school crush Isaac would be somewhere on this street selling the *Atalaya* magazine with his father. When she saw the girl with the sign, the blisters on her toes stung her into stopping in the middle of the sidewalk.

The young woman with the braids looked familiar, despite her kerchief and shirt. Her brown beret was slanted to the right side, held in place with black bobby pins, and it had a red patch with chocolate stitches spelling "La Causa" on the side.

Doña Goya stood in front of the girl, squinting, bobbing her head up and down. The young woman pushed her sign higher into the clear blue sky.

"Nice ass," a high school boy yelled, then laughed.

The girl kept pumping her sign toward the sky as if she wanted it to soar above the tangle of telephone lines and dingy buildings.

"Aren't you Lola's girl?" Doña Goya asked.

The girl said nothing, just lifted her eyes to the sky.

"Are you mute *o qué?*"

Cala pulled at her grandmother's elbow when she recognized the teen as Gabi, one of the neighbor's daughters. She had a distinctive scar on her temple. She was one of those students who would sit at the front of the class, always raising her hand whenever the teacher asked a question. In the school cafeteria, she would sit with the government nerds, talking about elections at school and in real life. Sometimes Cala would listen in. Gabi had urged Cala to join the high school's MEChA activist club, but Doña Goya refused to allow her to stay after school for the meetings, especially after she found out from her *comadre* Marta that it was the MEChistas who led the "blowouts" in the 1960s.

"Those MEChistas are troublemakers," she told Cala. "They blew up the schools twenty years ago."

Before she could stop herself, Cala twisted her mouth as Doña Goya raised her hand high for the hardest slap she would ever feel.

"Don't you twist your mouth at me," her grandmother said. "Most of those kids blowing up the schools were *comunistas y cholos desgraciados.*"

"They didn't blow up the schools," Cala said. "They walked out of their classrooms. That's what 'blow out' means."

"Where'd you learn that? At school?" Doña Goya asked.

"No. I saw it on TV," Cala said, realizing she never learned anything about the Chicano movement at school.

Instead of MEChA, Cala joined the California Scholarship Club and never spoke to Gabi again.

Now, Doña Goya got right in Gabi's face. "You should go to Mass, not stand out here in the street making trouble."

Gabi just kept thrusting her sign up, breathing hard through her kerchief. Sweat slid down from the edges of her felt beret onto her nose and into the folds of her bandana.

"The boycott's over, Dolores Huerta!" a man shouted from his pickup truck. Some boys snickered.

The sun beat down hard, but Doña Goya pulled her black *rebozo* tight around her head and shoulders as if it were rain and not the sun beating down. Then, just as she tried to reach up for Gabi's sign, Cala quickly jerked her arm back, and they both tumbled onto the sidewalk. Some shoppers formed a crowd around them. A tight circle of heads looked down.

"Are you okay?" Gabi asked, bending over Doña Goya and trying to help her up.

"Spoiled brat!" Goya yelled and slapped Gabi's face, loosening her beret.

Cala didn't know if her grandmother was yelling at her or Gabi. People stared as Doña Goya shakily stood up, berating Gabi, who slapped at the dirt and ashes on the old lady's skirt.

"She's hitting the old lady!" one of the high school boys yelled.

"No, she's not!" Cala screamed, scrambling to get herself up. "Leave us alone!"

Cala pulled Doña Goya away from the street corner and dragged her down to Thrifty's. She didn't see the boys who remained, circling Gabi, pushing her. One boy tore off her brown beret and flung it like a frisbee to another boy. Watching from across the street, the owner of La Malinche Botánica pulled her BB gun from under the counter. She quickly walked across the street, dodging the cars rolling down Whittier Boulevard. As soon as the drivers saw the BB gun, they slowed down and parted a path for her.

"Leave her alone!" The Malinche owner shouted, waving her gun at the teen boys surrounding Gabi.

As soon as the owner began shooting the BBs, the boys flew into the flowing crowds. Gabi knelt over her sign, braids loosened and her face flushed, and wiped the spit from her face that one of the boys had spewed at her. Quickly, the Malinche owner took Gabi across the street to her store, Gabi's fingers still clutching her homemade sign.

Inside La Malinche Botánica, the owner offered Gabi a cup of water. At first, Gabi shook her head, but when the owner moved the cup closer to her face, Gabi pulled off her bandana and drank. Her flushed face gradually cooled with the water and quiet darkness. The owner pulled a plastic orange chair from behind the counter. It reminded Gabi of a giant orange with its rounded plastic back. As soon as she leaned her sweaty back into the chair, she felt refreshed. Creosote-scented candle wax and incense filled her nostrils and wrapped gently around her throat and head.

"Thank you," Gabi said.

She noticed that the owner also wore her hair in braids. She looked like a Mexican hippie. Around her stood wooden statues of saints, traditional ones like San Martín de Porres and untraditional, like Jesús Malverde.

The owner offered her a wet paper towel. Gabi looked at the wet brown square for a few seconds, unable to understand it.

"To wipe your face," the owner said. Then, she nodded at Gabi's shirt and read, "*La Virgen rebelde.*"

Gabi wiped her face and patted her neck. She drank more water, then said she had to leave.

La Malinche's owner nodded and asked, "What's your name?"

"Gabi."

"Gabriela," the owner said, "like the archangel."

Gabi wiped her face again, then stood up.

"How'd you get that scar?" the owner asked.

Gabi's hand immediately flew to the bumpy flesh on her temple, instinctively rubbing it.

"I got caught stealing some tortillas from JonSon's," Gabi said. "I was running, then I fell in the parking lot . . . slipped on oil and fell on one of those cement parking things."

"Tortillas?"

"For my mom," Gabi said, looking straight into the owner's face. "Dad was on strike."

"Where does he work?"

"Long Beach," Gabi said. "He's a steelworker."

"Hold on a minute," the store owner said as she rifled through her many wooden drawers. "So, while dad strikes, you steal tortillas to feed the family. Like Robin Hood," the owner approved, nodding. "Like Jesús Malverde."

"Who's that?"

"Here," the owner said, holding a tiny shadow box. "For protection."

It was a bust of Jesús Malverde tied to a waxed leather cord. Gabi looked down at the face of a mustachioed man in a green shirt and a delicately drawn black tie.

"He stole from the rich and gave to the poor. Do the same."

"I don't give away money," she said.

The owner's eyes closed and she bowed her head. "Other things have value . . . like a tortilla."

Gabi smiled. She looked around the darkened store filled to the brim with candles, plaster statues of saints and jars of herbs and powders. The semi-darkness of the store cooled her head and dried the sweat from her scalp. She patted her braids, loosened by the boy who had ripped off her beret.

"Here," the owner said, handing her a brush.

Slowly, Gabi undid her braids, then redid them, pulling each interlacing strand tight until her scalp hurt.

⤲ ⤳

Outside Thrifty's drugstore, Cala recognized her high school crush standing alongside an older man. It was her next-door neighbor, Isaac, the boy whose father would force him to practice the accordion in his front yard while all the neighborhood kids watched, laughed and sometimes threw rocks at him. Across their chests, Isaac and his father held copies of *Atalaya* magazine. As soon as Isaac saw her, he fled into the store to hide in one of the many aisles. His father immediately went in after him.

Doña Goya noticed Isaac's father chase him down. "This is why we're Catholic. *Pinches Testigos de Jehová.*"

Inside the drugstore, shoppers, churchgoers and their children snaked against the greeting card wall stacked with brightly colored Easter cards. Cala had nearly lost her appetite, but she still craved the cold sweetness of the coconut and pineapple ice cream that the drugstore served.

"Fat and pimples," her grandmother said. "That's all that ice cream will do for you. A *raspado* would have been better."

"I'd like it on a sugar cone, please," Cala told the server, a pimply boy with wire-rimmed glasses and a white paper hat.

Doña Goya rolled her eyes and pulled her black *rebozo* tight around her head. Cala knew she'd never hear the end of her grandmother's complaints.

Just as Cala handed her money over to the cashier, she saw Isaac running from his father. He ran past her, and Cala decided to drop her ice cream cone in front of his father, who slipped and slid across the speckled linoleum floor. Isaac's father grabbed Doña Goya's shoulder to keep himself from falling, pulling Doña Goya down to the ground for the second time that afternoon. Isaac's father crashed against the greeting card rack. Seeing his chance, Isaac threw open the glass doors and ran down Whittier Boulevard.

"See what you did!" Doña Goya hissed at Cala from the floor.

Cala did not hear a word. All she knew was that she had sacrificed her beloved pineapple and coconut ice cream to help Isaac escape public humiliation at Thrifty's. Later, as they walked home, Doña Goya's constant murmuring as she limped shadowed her like a ghost.

"Spoiled brat," her grandmother repeated.

This time Cala knew she was the target of her grandmother's ire. Suddenly, she remembered Gabi's sign. Being a good Mexican girl in America seemed to be a myth now.

The next day, Doña Goya murmured endless prayers for the Virgen and curses for Cala for letting her fall. Cala ignored her as she slapped a flour tortilla onto one of the stove's burners, noticing the brilliant orange bursts in between the cold blue flames. As the thick tortilla swelled, its stiffness softened over the flames. Cala grew hungrier. She snatched it from the flames before Doña Goya could start another one of her prayers or curses and headed out the door.

On her way to school, Cala saw Gabi walking ahead of her. She was still wearing braids, but this time they were entwined with red, white and green ribbons that gleamed in the morning sun. She was wearing a red shirt with an eagle on the back of it. Over her left shoulder hung a black backpack heavy with books. The cement sidewalks blazed in the sunny April morning. Punkers, headbangers, nerds, mods, preppies, GQ guys and cha-cha girls flowed alongside Cala and Gabi. No *cholos* except for those cruising "low and slow" around the school, blasting the KRLA songs "Angel Baby" and "I'm Your Puppet." They checked out the "fresh meat": girls or potential new gang members or maybe old friends left behind when the principal had kicked the gangbangers out of school. At least that was the rumor.

Throughout the morning, Cala noticed Gabi in class and in the hallways. In their AP European history class, Gabi didn't raise her hand the way she usually did, not even when Mr. Bennet asked for a volunteer to read the passage on France's emperor taking over Mexico. Nor did Gabi offer any analysis about imperialism in the Belgian Congo and dehumanization of Africans in *Heart of Darkness* for AP English Lit. Gabi didn't do anything, not until lunchtime. While Cala was standing in the burger hash line with her friend Alma, "Born in East LA" played over the loudspeakers set up on a shaded table at the center of the mall. Cala rolled her eyes. She hated that song, but that was the number one request, so what could she do? Why didn't they play something cool like "West End Girls" by the Pet Shop Boys or "Planet Earth" by Duran Duran? Cala and Alma carried their cardboard boxes of cafeteria burgers and French fries to a shaded spot under one of the mulberry trees that circled the grassy mall.

She had just started on her story about Isaac and his father, when Cala saw Gabi trudging up to the center of the grassy mall. Despite her heavy backpack, she leaped like a ballet dancer over the low brick wall surrounding the mall. She strode to the center of the lawn area and pulled the cord from the speaker, cutting Bruce Springsteen off in the middle of yowling "I'm Going Down." From her backpack, Gabi pulled out a brown felt roll. Quickly, she flapped it open. It was a sign with the words "Blow Out" stitched with yellow lettering. Chitter chatter quieted down as Gabi held the sign above her head, slowly rotating, making sure everyone could read her sign as well as see the red shirt with the black image of the UFW pyramid eagle and the words "Huelga Now."

Alma looked puzzled. Cala had not told her about Gabi's sign on Whittier Boulevard. What for? They never hung out with her, anyway. Gabi was a suck-up, a teacher's pet. But today, Gabi did not listen to the approaching teachers and the counselors, who reprimanded her, squawking like crows. After one of them pulled away her sign, she held up her fist. Some students laughed, others shrugged and continued eating their lunch. The felt cloth fluttered on the grass like a resting butterfly. Its gold letters gleaming in the bright spring sun.

"Nobody cares anyway," Alma said between hamburger bites. "Check it out."

She flicked a fry in Gabi's direction. Other students started following suit. Soon, more students started throwing ketchup packets, apples and some even threw pebbles.

For a moment, Cala thought about joining Gabi on the hill. Before she could step up, the principal flanked by two narcs strode across the courtyard to the grassy mall. He started speaking to her before he grabbed her fist and twisted her arm behind her back. The mall got quiet. Gabi started squirming but stopped as soon as Principal Duplessis twisted harder.

Gabi flinched but looked around and started shouting. "Can't you see?"

She made eye contact with Cala, who couldn't look away.

"Can't you see what's going on! Wake up!"

A small image of a man with a mustache and green shirt hung from a leather cord around her neck. Cala recognized

Jesús Malverde from the little altar her grandmother had at the top of her chest of drawers.

Cala froze. Nobody helped Gabi, not the MEChistas, not the few sympathetic teachers, nobody, as the narcs cuffed Gabi and took her back to Duplessis' office.

"I got rid of the *cholos*," Duplessis said in a voice loud enough for Cala to hear as they walked by. "I can get rid of you."

"She should've kept her mouth shut," Alma said as they walked to their lockers. "We're living in the 80s, not the 60s."

Cala pulled out her books and binder for AP Calculus. She just wasn't in the mood for derivatives, but she went to class anyway because Isaac would be there. He never missed a class. But when Mr. Escalante shut the classroom door, Isaac's chair was empty.

❧ ❧

In the principal's office, Gabi held on to her Jesús Malverde pendant, rubbing it while the principal called her mother at work. At first, he called the number listed on her permanent record, but when that didn't work, Gabi gave him another number, the one she found stuck underneath Malverde's bust.

"Is this Gabi's mother?" Duplessis asked. Then, in broken Spanglish, he said, "*Soy el* director *de escola.*"

The voice of the owner of La Malinche Botánica murmured like a prayer through the receiver. Above Gabi, a metal fan slowly rotated, barely ventilating the small high-ceilinged office that faced south towards Sixth Street. In the distance, Gabi could barely make out La Malinche Botánica.

"Gabriela no school," Duplessis told the owner. "*Siete días.*"

"Okay," the owner said.

To stifle her giggles, Gabi bent her head between her knees and took deep breaths. When she looked up, Duplessis was sitting at the edge of his oak desk.

"I know what you were trying to do, and it's not going to work," Duplessis said.

He offered her a cup of water from the Sparkletts dispenser in his office. Gabi shook her head, her face calm. Just then, the rest of the MEChA club showed up at his office, their eyes hooded, mouths tight. Duplessis looked straight at Gabi.

"Thanks to you, MEChA will no longer exist here," Duplessis continued. "When you come back, you can join another group but not this one."

≈∙≈

After school, as Cala walked to the school's front gates, a group of students wearing brown berets were marched out of the school by the two narcs that had helped Duplessis handcuff Gabi. At the gate, some met their parents. One boy flipped off the narc, threw his beret at him and ran all the way down to Whittier Boulevard. It was Isaac. Cala's heart throbbed. How could he have joined MEChA without her knowing?

As soon as she passed the gates, Cala ran home. She pounded on the door, but Doña Goya did not answer. She was probably still making her way back from the Santuario de Guadalupe. Cala frantically keyed the lock to the heavy wooden front door and burst into the living room. Her chest tightened. She placed her hands on her knees and bent over to keep from feeling dizzy. After a couple of deep breaths, Cala closed her eyes. When she opened them, she noticed a stiff fry stuck to her pant leg. Cala squeezed her eyes shut, but the image of Gabi's black eagle against a red sky burned into her eyelids. She went straight to her grandmother's bed-room. The wide-open door filled with the bright light pump-ing through the window. On top of the bureau, Jesús Malverde stared back at her. The bust of a young man with a skinny mustache and dulled eyes rested next to the plaster statue of the Virgen de Guadalupe.

Suddenly, she heard Doña Goya coming in the front door. Cala swiftly climbed over her grandmother's bed, out the bedroom door and into the one bathroom they shared. She flushed the toilet and ran the faucet for a few seconds.

"How was the church?"

"Horrible," her grandmother said as she turned on the black and white TV in the kitchen.

Immediately, the glowing face of Walter Mercado filled the screen. "Those priests are so lazy. They can't even clean the altar by themselves."

Doña Goya went to the refrigerator and pulled out yes-terday's refried beans. Cala walked back to the living room to pick up her backpack. Instead of taking it to the kitchen as she usually did, she carried it to her bedroom. She turned on her small black and white TV and watched a faint picture emerge from the grey tube. It was Cheech Marin singing "Born in East LA." Instinctively, she reached for the dial, but Cala forced herself to watch the video. She braced herself against the stereotypes but nevertheless found herself laughing at them.

"What's so funny? Did you hear about the neighbor's daughter? La Gabi" Doña Goya asked eagerly as she sat her-self down next to Cala.

"Yes," Cala said, turning down the volume.

"She'll probably end up in jail like the other *cholas*."

The next day, Doña Goya walked Cala to school to make sure Gabi didn't bother her. Doña Goya wore her black every-day *rebozo* over her head and over her black blouse and navy skirt. She was wearing matching black socks and the "nurse" shoes she had bought at the CHOC second-hand store down the street. The cool April morning vibrated with chatter and music booming from cars cruising up the street towards the school's gates. Students, parents, cops walked, talked, drove as if nothing had happened yesterday.

"Gabi's never bothered me," Cala said, rolling her eyes.

As they passed Gabi's house, Cala half-expected to see her braided head peer out through the curtains. She wondered what Gabi would do all day.

"Is that her?" Doña Goya said, pointing her chin at a pick-up truck with two women who were laughing and smoking cigarettes. "I'm Your Puppet" was blaring out their lowered windows.

"No," Cala said, but she thought she saw Isaac in the back-seat.

Walking quickly, she tried to leave Doña Goya behind, but her grandmother clung to her arm, keeping her pace slower than the other students walking towards Garfield.

At the gate, Doña Goya finally let her go, although Cala could feel her grandmother's eyes watching her. She turned around before she entered the building with the tiled Aztec calendar on its side and waved back. As soon as Doña Goya walked off, Cala jogged straight to her locker. Rolled and stowed away in the back of the locker, was Gabi's chocolate brown felt sign, the one the teacher had dropped on the grass during lunch time. In the cool steel of the locker, its yellow letters glowed in the dim fluorescent light of the hallway. After pulling her books for AP Spanish, Cala slammed the locker shut before Alma showed up.

Later that day, while the speakers boomed "Take on Me" at lunchtime, Cala unfurled the sign, stood at the top of the hill and waited for Isaac and Gabi to join her.

How to Tell a True East LA Story

First of all, forget about the gangs, the cops and the caca that comes out of Hollywood about East LA, or East Los, as we locals like to call it. East Los is all about little old ladies, *abuelitas* watering their lawns at five in the afternoon, waving to their neighbors, trying to dig out the latest gossip from their neighbors.

It's about a neighbor's roosters crowing for four hours starting at 4 am. It's about walking home from school and stopping by the corner grocery store owned by *chinitos* who make the best cherry *raspados* in the world.

It's about Mexican Mexicans who work at anything, such as selling frozen fruit bars in 90-degree heat or working in sweatshops to wire back money to their wives, kids and parents stuck in little *pueblitos*.

Sometimes it's about cats, Dinah Shore and grandmothers. I'm talking about my *comadre* Magdalena, the hairstylist at César's Palace, whose *abuela*, Grandma Fina, visited her as a cat on the Day of the Dead.

"Swear to God," Magdalena says. She was sitting in her patio, enjoying the moonlight with a shot of tequila, when she heard singing. At first Magdalena thought it was her neighbor playing the radio too loud, but no, it was this fat cat with orange eyes and fur as red-orange as Grandma Fina's.

"Was that you singing?" Magdalena asked.

"Of course. Listen up."

The cat sang "*La Llorona*" à la Chavela Vargas all the way through. And that's a tough song with all its high notes and long llooooooorooooooonaaaaaaas. Magdalena swore she could hear guitars and *guitarrones* strumming and humming, as she approached her house. She got so scared when she got home, she ran into the kitchen, but Grandma Fina slipped in through the door before she could shut it.

That was Grandma Fina's first visit since her death last year. Nobody went to grandma's funeral except for Magdalena and me. Then Magdalena set up the altar because she thought it would make Fina feel better. I told her not to do it. I may be an atheist but I don't believe in taking chances, especially after Grandpa Laureano's last visit. Since she's still somewhat *católica*, Magdalena thought she owed it to Grandma Fina because her mother Rosa didn't even go to the funeral, wouldn't even visit Fina when she was dying in the hospital. Now she was back.

Grandma Fina jumped to the top of her altar, stepping her fat orange body between the candles, plates of *chiles rellenos* and ashtrays holding Winston cigarettes.

"Back in my day, only the *indios* celebrated their dead," Grandma Fina said, sniffing the little sugar skulls. She made a stink face when she got to the Mexican marigolds.

"Don't give me that face," Magdalena said. "The cigarettes stink more than those *cempasúchiles*."

All her life, Magdalena's mom Rosa always told her about how Grandma Fina hated her and Grandpa Laureano. How after Laureano died, strange men never stopped visiting Fina. How Fina dumped her in an orphanage and then brought her back to do all the cooking and cleaning. Magdalena and I always remembered her drinking tequila and cooking the best *chiles rellenos* whenever we visited her out there in Boyle

Heights. Her house was tiny, tiny with a yellow kitchen, blue bedroom, little bitty patio filled with plants in clay pots and tin coffee cans. In the kitchen, there was always some guy either sitting at the table or on the couch in the living room under lots of photos of children, grandchildren, godchildren and loved ones, including Rosa looking like Mary Tyler Moore in a flip hairdo. Grandma Fina always had some boyfriend lurking around her house. I remember this guy, Rutilio, who always wore his cowboy hat, grey slacks and black shiny shoes. He'd always sit straight up, stiff with age.

"Whatever happened to that guy?" Magdalena asked me one time.

"She replaced him with Alfredo, Pedro or some other *fulano*," I said.

"Why didn't she marry him?"

"Because he couldn't get it up?" Magdalena ventured. "Nah, probably a womanizer."

"*Mensa*," Grandma Fina meows. "It was because I was *católica*."

Magdalena tilted her head, confused.

"He was still married," Grandma Fina says, stretching and licking her leg. "His wife was back in a little *pueblito* in Zacatecas."

Besides her many gentlemen, there were always at least ten cats on Fina's patio eating from little paper plates or drinking water from glass bowls. There was Monina, Tonchito, Joe, Pati and so many others I can't remember.

"All my kids," she'd say when she was alive. "These are all my kids, too."

So now she came back as a cat, ready to drink more tequila, sing and check out the fancy altar set up for her.

Suddenly, Grandma Fina jumped down from the altar and walked over to Magdalena.

"What I wouldn't give for just a little sip of tequila."

I think maybe Magdalena was drinking a little too much, but she tells me that after hearing her grandma's scratchy voice come out of the cat, she sobered up real pronto.

"But you're a cat. Cats don't like tequila," Magdalena said, trying to find the rosary she kept near the little altar to the Virgencita beside the window.

"Never mind that. Gimme a sip."

Magdalena put the little shot glass adorned with a red sombrero down on the floor. It was Fina's favorite when she was alive. Fina sniffed it a little, then stuck her black tongue slowly into the tequila. She looked at Magdalena, squinted her copper eyes, licked her nose and started lapping it up.

"*Válgame Dios*, Grandma! You're gonna get sick all over my floor."

"Don't forget I have a liver made of iron," Grandma Fina purred. "Besides, I died of lung cancer, not cirrhosis!"

Fina delicately walked over the rest of the altar smelling, sometimes licking the flowers, the *panes de muerto*, the bowls filled with water. Suddenly, she stopped in front of the small portrait of Grandpa Laureano.

"Why did you put up that picture of Grandpa?" Fina asked, swatting the frame. "He irritated the hell out of me. I think he's the one who killed me, not my lungs."

"How was I supposed to know that? And who else am I going to put up there?"

"How about a picture of Rogelio García?"

"The fruit guy?"

"Yes. We had a thing going on, but don't tell Rosa. She'll have a heart attack."

"Where'd you learn about Día de los Muertos?" Grandma Fina asked while chewing on a cigarette filter.

Magdalena told her about our fifth-grade teacher, Miss Rogers (sorry, *Ms.* Rogers), who taught us about this Mexican holiday that none of us had ever heard of, even though we were all Mexican kids. Of course, except for a few, most of the kids were born and bred here in LA. As far as we knew, we were Americans. And our parents made sure we kept the *mexicanadas* to a minimum. So, when "Miz" Rogers showed us pictures of *indios* in Oaxaca decorating cement tombs with hundreds of orange flowers, candles and *panes de muerto* on the big white screen that hung over the blackboard, we were blown away.

Magdalena and I looked at each other. We had to do this! Her Grandpa Laureano had just died alone in Juárez and, since Rosa couldn't get the time off to go to his funeral, this do-it-yourself ritual would have to do. When Magdalena told her mother Rosa that we wanted to cover the kitchen table with flowers and candles to honor her Grandpa Laureano, Rosa laughed; then, after thinking about our request, she scrunched up her face.

"Go ahead, but you better clean up this table before you go to bed," she told us. "And you better blow out all the candles. I don't want any fires. I paid a lot for this house."

That night, after cleaning up the table and making sure all the candles had been blown out, Magdalena and I went into a deep sleep. I slept until the smell of Rosa's pancakes and frying bacon woke me up the next morning. Rosa always made them on Sundays when she didn't have to work at the battery factory in Vernon. Because Día de los Muertos fell on a Sunday, it was a doubly holy day. While we brushed our teeth, Magdalena told me Grandpa Laureano had visited her while I slept.

"Stop lying," I told her as she poured Mrs. Butterworth's syrup over the steaming pancakes. She was starting to scare me.

"For reals," she said, not touching the pancakes or the crispy bacon.

I smothered my bacon in syrup while she talked about waking up in the middle of the night to the sound of the phone receiver in the living room shaking in its cradle.

"How come I didn't hear it?" I asked.

"You were snoring."

"I don't snore!" I yelled. I was scared but I wanted to know more. "Then what happened?"

"The dishes," Magdalena said as she pointed to them sitting in a plastic rack beside the sink.

"What about the dishes?"

All at once Magdalena stood up and went to the rack and with both hands moved them back and forth.

"They were shaking and moving back and forth by themselves," she said, pushing them until one of the dishes fell and bounced off onto the thick linoleum floor.

Rosa's shoulders shook with laughter while she poured the batter over the hot *comal.* She was laughing so hard that instead of perfectly round pancakes, they looked like giant commas and S's. Rosa didn't say anything until Magdalena said she thought Grandpa Laureano was trying to reach her.

"Don't tell your grandma that," Rosa said, pouring the last of the batter.

"Why not?" Magdalena asked.

"You'll scare her," Rosa said.

But now I think it's because Grandma Fina didn't want anything more to do with Grandpa Laureano. Maybe this was why she came back to visit Magdalena, to set her straight about her feelings about him, Rutilio, Rogelio and the other men in her life.

With her thick furry paws, Grandma Fina climbed up to the very top of the altar and sniffed the picture of herself as a young *pachuca*, slow dancing with this *pachuco* in a zoot suit.

"*Ay*, how I miss that dress," she said, rubbing the frame. "I used to wear it every Friday night when I got together with my *carnalas*. We used to go out dancing. Sometimes they put on these amateur nights, we could go up and sing, dance or do some old comedy act. You know your great-aunt Roselia and I used to win prizes singing at the theaters?"

Magdalena couldn't imagine her chain-smoking *abuela* and *tía abuela* Roselia singing with their scratchy old-lady voices. But then again, Fina did belt out "La Llorona" better than Chavela Vargas ever could. Magdalena laughed loud and hard at the thought.

"Don't laugh," she meowed. "I could've been famous if I hadn't been so stupid."

Suddenly, she jumped out the window and back into the darkness. Before Magdalena knew it, Fina came running back with a big envelope and shook it open. Yellowed newspaper clippings, photos and letters fell onto the linoleum.

One of the headlines read, "Mexican Girls Beat Out Dinah Shore in Singing Competition." Below that was a picture of two girls with their mouths open in big, black O's.

A sister act beat out the great Dinah Shore last night at the Orpheum, a Spanish movie house just east of Los Angeles. The sisters García received the longest standing ovation and won $10. This was their 10th win. The standout was Josephine García, whose rendition of "Bésame mucho" wowed the crowd and overshadowed Miss Shore's performance of "Sentimental Journey."

"But I thought Mom said you worked the bars downtown."

"Well, it's time you knew the real story."

"How come Tía Roselia never mentioned it?"

"Because she wasn't the one who beat out Dinah Shore."

Now, the cat sat down in Magdalena's lap, purring away as if it was perfectly normal. Magdalena did not seem scared anymore, mainly because she pressed her rosary against Grandma Fina's fur and it didn't set her on fire. She figured if this talking fat cat could touch the *rosario*, then maybe she was not some devil.

"So what happened? Why didn't you end up rich and famous instead of Dinah?"

"Aah, in those days, no Mexicans were famous. You had to look like Rita Hayworth or Dolores del Río. I was too ugly and poor. Looked too much like an *india*."

"Is that why you drank?"

"Sometimes. Sometimes I drank because I just didn't know what else to do."

"And Amá? Why does she hate you so much?"

"I was a shitty mom. No big secret. I married Laureano when I really wanted to sing and travel. That's just how I was when I was younger."

Grandma Fina stayed until the next day and told Magdalena all kinds of family secrets, secrets that Magdalena won't let me in on. That's okay. Maybe they're true. Maybe they're not.

So I took whatever Magdalena's told me and turned it into a movie script. I thought, maybe I could sell it to this producer I know at Miramax, where I work as an assistant. All I do is run errands for these assholes, and in LA that's no easy feat, considering that I have to hop on at least five different freeways from Hollywood to the San Fernando Valley or to Santa Monica. At least my trusty Honda has air conditioning and a working radio, not bad for a twenty-year-old car. Besides driving every freeway to pick up dry cleaning or set up locations, I have to put up with these idiots who think they're so smooth but are old enough to be my grandfather. One old asshole comes in for the morning meeting at the production office and nags me every day for my phone number. He thinks he's real suave, but he's just gross. *¡Qué asco!*

So, I decided to talk to one of the head honchos, a Chicano producer who used to write for big time TV shows like *Friends* and *Chico and the Man*. Now "Paco" was producing for Miramax, so I showed him my script about Magdalena's "encounter" with Grandma Fina. All he said was that nobody would believe a talking cat who's somebody's grandma.

"Maybe if you make Magdalena into a prostitute or maybe some kind of *chola*?" he said, while he chewed on the *pan dulce* I had bought him all the way from El Gallo on First Street.

He's gotta be kidding.

"But how do people believe a Puerto Rican and a white old man can run a garage in East LA?" I ask. "Or that there are no black or brown people in New York City? How's that real?"

"That's true," he laughs. "*Pero, m'ija . . .*"

I hated it when he called me *m'ija*. I may have been thirty-one but I had my degree and my own car. True, I still lived with my parents and sisters, but I was a grown woman, not some dumb kid.

"You gotta know," Paco continued, "Hollywood's not about 'realness.' If you don't get that, you're never gonna make it here."

"No self-respecting Chicano's gonna work for a racist white guy," I say, getting angrier.

Paco laughs harder, louder.

"As long as there's a white guy in the picture," he says, trying to catch his breath, "then Hollywood's gonna go for it."

Later, I talked to a Miramax writer, a Chicana who wrote for *Culture Clash* about this Hollywood realness caca.

"*Mira*," she says, shaking her head, "that's what they want, bullshit, Hollywood-style 'realness.'"

She thought all these other writers and producers were dumber than a box of rocks, and she didn't laugh at me.

So much for Miramax, the supposedly "cutting edge" studio in Hollywood. This is Magdalena's story, and it's more real than all the shit those Hollywood *cabrones* put out about our barrio. Whatever. I'll shop my little script around for some independent production company. Maybe I'll set up my own altar next time.

Gracias and Acknowledgements

I would like to express my heartfelt gratitude and *cariño* to my husband for his unwavering support and to my *familia* for their inspiration.

My deepest appreciation to Dr. Nicolás Kanellos and the amazing staff at Arte Público Press for their diligence and faith in my book.

Thank you to my friends who lent their ears, eyes and most importantly their hearts to me during my writing and editing process: Monique, Cindy, Wanda, Veronica, Karen and Charlie. *¡Gracias por todo!*

For literary space and sustenance, I cannot thank the following writing groups enough: Escritorx, Las Guayabas, Sowing the Seeds and Mujeres Que Escriben.

I am grateful to the following *chingona* writers for their encouragement, vision and voice: Helena María Viramontes, Sandra Cisneros, Edwidge Danticat, Leslie Marmon Silko, Ai, Murasaki Shikibu, Dorothy Allison and Jane Austen. You are my literary *comadres* and I am indebted to you.

Throughout my writing career, I have been fortunate to learn from extraordinary teachers and editors. I would like to express my boundless appreciation to Meg Files, the first writing teacher and author to say "yes" to my fiction and poetry. *Abrazotes para Daniel Olivas,* poet and editor extraor-

e who anthologized my first story. Many thanks to the .rkable and tireless Laura Pegram whose patience nur-:d an embryonic narrative into a fully developed story.

To the writers and readers I met at Pima Writers' Work-лop, The Pasadena Writing Project, University of Arizona Poetry Center, Cornell University and VONA, thank you for your inspiration and guidance.

I would like to acknowledge the editors and publishers of the following journals and anthologies in which versions of these stories first appeared and, in some cases, "reappeared:" *Kaleidescope*, "Chola Salvation;" *Lotusland: An Anthology of Contemporary Southern California Literature* and *Eleven Eleven*, "Act of Faith;" *Aster(ix)* and *Huizache*, "Powder Puff;" *Kweli Journal*, "Angry Blood;" *La Bloga* and *SandScript*, "Pepper Spray" and *Pasadena Weekly*, "I Hate My Name."

A big salute to the *Pushcart Prize* committee for recognizing "Angry Blood" with a "Special Mention." Thank you to Best American Non-Required Reading for selecting "Powder Puff" as a "Notable Nonrequired Reading."

A huge *gracias* to Alia Phibes, aka Evilkid, for her beautiful portrait of the *virgencita* as a *chingona chola*. How did you know?

I am also grateful to the numerous American, Mexican and British music artists of the 70s, 80s and 90s whose music provided the soundtrack to my stories before I ever wrote them.

Finally, to the *gente*, places and spirit of East LA, *mil gracias y ¡mucho, mucho amor!*